METATRON

ELYON'S WARRIORS

EVE LANGLAIS

Copyright Metatron © Eve Langlais

Cover Art © Covers by Julie

Produced in Canada

Published by Eve Langlais

http://www.EveLanglais.com

eBook: ISBN: 978 177 384 4503

Print ISBN: 978 177 384 4510

ALL RIGHTS RESERVED

This book is a work of fiction and the characters, events and dialogue found within the story are of the author's imagination and are not to be construed as real. Any resemblance to actual events or persons, either living or deceased, is completely coincidental.

No part of this book may be reproduced or shared in any form or by any means, electronic or mechanical, including but not limited to digital copying, file sharing, audio recording, email and printing without permission in writing from the author.

FOREWORD

A long time ago, God planted seeds on Earth and they grew to be humanity. This flock was tended and watched over by a choir of angels from their ark. Only, the inhabitants they herded weren't very obedient. As a matter of fact, they questioned and even killed their shepherds.

Despite this, the surviving choir did their best to maintain order and to convince the flock to obey the commandments given to them by God. Perhaps, had the angels not been overrun by greed and warring forces, they might have remained in control.

Instead, the angels were eradicated by the humans and forgotten by God.

Eons passed and a new choir of angels rediscovered the lost colony, but so has Hell. The forces of darkness and chaos are coming to pillage Earth and will kill billions with their greed.

FOREWORD

A good thing Angels aren't only peacekeepers but fierce warriors full of righteous fury—and an ability to love.

PROLOGUE

A*TTEND ME AT ONCE.*

When God commanded, angels had no choice but to listen, hence why Metatron dropped his training duties and now stood before Elyon, who sat upon his mighty throne. Metatron waited.

And waited.

A good thing patience happened to be a virtue he possessed in plenty, because Elyon did so enjoy playing games. Especially ones to showcase his power.

Metatron already had an idea of why he'd been called before God. He hadn't been the most obedient of angels lately. Not that he'd done anything overt. Only visiting an angel being held prisoner in Dante's Inferno and giving that captive a clue to escape. Not stripping the wings from insubordinates but rather banishing them to planets out of sight of a vengeful deity. But his most insidious crime? Not fawning at Elyon's feet. He'd never been the type to fall prostate, but what little respect he'd once held for Heaven's God had long since dissipated.

The deity in question sat ramrod straight on his throne, a frothy moving concoction of clouds that somehow held his weight. As appearances went, Elyon's changed depending on his mood. Sometimes being that of a young fit male with muscled physique and square jaw. Other times, he chose an older façade, replete with long white beard and flowing robes. Only one thing never changed: the glowing eyes. Angels could sometimes project a soft brilliance with their orbs, but it never lasted long. Elyon, however, because of the power he wielded, could never truly hide amongst his flocks, hence why he had scions to do his bidding.

When Elyon finally deigned to acknowledge Metatron, his blank expression suddenly animating as he returned to his physical form, Metatron braced himself. Elyon could be temperamental and had been known to smite for small slights. Just in case, Metatron stayed ready to fling up a shield if necessary. Could he win in a direct fight with God? Not with the power Elyon commanded, but at the same time, Metatron wielded a sword better than anyone. He might prevail if he was fast enough, but he kept such mutinous thoughts veiled from Elyon. A trick he'd long ago learned to avoid the nosy mind-poking of a paranoid deity.

"You disappoint me, Metatron." God's voice, while low, still echoed in the vast chamber. The throne room spanned several stories and had a fluted shape, which Metatron had long suspected amplified Elyon's metaphysical ability to speak across long distances.

"Apologies, Your Holiness." He dipped his head in feigned contrition. Metatron had learned how to handle Elyon when he got in a mood. "I will pray for your forgiveness and strive to do better so that I might return to your good grace."

Elyon snorted. "I see we can add lying to your many faults."

"Angels can't lie." Not entirely false. Most really couldn't. Their vows to Heaven and, more specifically, Elyon prevented it. But Metatron wasn't like the others. Blame age and experience for the fact he could do and feel things others couldn't.

"We both know you're more than a simple angel." A disgruntled reply. "You should have long ago moved on from your archangel status if not for your constant need to vex me."

Metatron held in a grimace at the thought of becoming part of Elyon's sycophant inner circle. "I have no interest in being anything more than your loyal soldier."

"You make that claim, and yet you're undermining my authority."

"In what way?" Metatron played innocent.

"Removing dissidents before they can be punished."

"Banishing them, Your Holiness, that you might concentrate on more important things." Metatron hated needless death. An angel shouldn't have to die because they chafed at Elyon's strict rules.

"Always with the quick replies. Do you think I'm blind to your plotting? I know you're behind it."

"Behind what?" He truly didn't know what Elyon spoke of, but imagined it had to do with his growing paranoia that Heaven, and his flocks, conspired to take him down. Metatron had given the rebellion some thought, but never anything more because, without God, Heaven would crumble.

"Do you think me blind and stupid?" God boomed, rising from his chair and growing in stature to become twice Metatron's size. "Your insubordination will not be tolerated."

"Will you smite me, then?" Metatron couldn't contain himself. He'd been taught since the creche to always be honest. And while a lie might keep him alive, he couldn't hold his tongue. "If I'm defying some of your commands, then perhaps it is because they are at odds with the holy laws you enacted and have your warriors upholding."

"*My* laws!" Elyon spat. "Which means I can

change them if I wish. And if I give you a command, you are to obey it at once."

Another angel might have been blubbering on the floor, promising to do better, begging for another chance. Metatron shook his head. "I am not a mindless puppet. I have a conscience guided by my faith, and I won't do anything to tarnish it." On this, Metatron wouldn't back down. To think there used to be a time when he loved and respected God. Would have done anything for him. What happened to Elyon? Or had Metatron simply been too blinded by devotion before to see him as he truly was? A being with too much power who decided he was above his own laws.

"Blasphemer," hissed Elyon, sitting back down.

"There was a time you valued my words and suggestions. What happened?"

"You have become weak. Influenced most likely by Hell's insidious taint on the worlds you've visited."

Elyon might have a point. Had Metatron changed? In some respects, yes, but at the same time, at his core, he remained a loyal servant to Heaven, just maybe not God anymore. "I am Heaven's loyal servant."

"A nice way of avoiding saying you are obedient to me." Elyon zeroed in on his choice of words. "Your attitude poses a dilemma."

"My attitude?" Once more, Metatron couldn't

hold his tongue. "Perhaps the question you should ask instead is, why have *you* strayed from the holy path? Where is the kind and compassionate God I once served?"

"You understand nothing!" God's reply came with a tightening of Metatron's throat, as if an invisible fist held it. "What I do, I do for Heaven."

Metatron flexed his fists and broke the hold on him, not easily, and he knew very well Elyon could have tightened the grip and snapped his neck had he wanted to. "If you have a plan or a vision, then tell me that I might understand your commands."

"I don't have to explain myself to you or anyone else. I would smite you, but that might cause more issues than your death would merit. What am I to do with you?" Elyon drummed his fingers on his throne. "Take your wings?"

The idea horrified. "On what grounds?"

"Because I said so," Elyon retorted. "But again, that might make you a martyr, and that won't do. I need you out of sight, fading from people's minds." God leaned back on his throne, the clouds shifting to accommodate, and a smile touched his lips. "A mission, far from here, would accomplish that. And lucky for you, I have a cantorii ready for departure."

"Going to banish me to a colony planet?" Metatron spat. He should have been rejoicing he'd live, but the rude reward for being a loyal warrior stung.

"The current planets are already taken care of.

It's time we expanded. Therefore, you will embark on a journey of exploration. It is time we probe and seed the far-flung reaches of the universe."

In other words, permanent exile. God's way of handling a messy situation. He couldn't kill Metatron, not without just cause. Stripping him of his wings and HALO would also draw notice, as Metatron's bravery and service to Heaven were well documented.

But this, sending him off on a futile search, far from Heaven... Perhaps it wasn't the worst thing that could happen. In fact, it could be the perfect solution to get him away from Elyon and finally forge a life for himself, free of the constant wars and conflicts.

The expulsion was how Metatron ended up principality of a cantorii that ventured into a spiral galaxy, where they found the lost colony of Eden.

It was also where he'd most likely die because Hell was on its doorstep.

CHAPTER 1

Sometime before Aziel got caught on camera, Zakai found Atlantis, and Elija destroyed Astaroth's castle...

The day I met an angel I happened to be drunk. In my defense, I'd had a terrible week. My boss fired me from my receptionist job at a car dealership so he could give my spot to his mistress. My car died on the way home and the tow truck wouldn't give me a lift, so I had to walk a few miles in the pouring rain only to get to my place—an attic apartment that overlooked a parking lot—and find the ceiling leaking. Not just drips of water, but a torrent that led to my landlord telling me to leave for my own safety.

I barely managed to pack a bag before I got shoved out of my place. With no paycheck coming in and little savings, I couldn't exactly afford a hotel, and I hated mooching off friends. Not having many alternatives, I turned to the only place I could access and not have to pay: the church basement we used to host our Templar Knights meetings.

Yes, I said Templar Knights, a secretive society whose stated purpose was fighting Hell's minions, but in reality, it was more an excuse to meet up, have drinks, and chat about how the world sucked and had strayed from God's path. The weird part about me being a member? I wasn't very religious. I inherited my spot because of my father and his father before him. A whole line of sons stretching way back and ending in me.

A woman.

Luckily, being an only daughter led to my dad not being a misogynistic ass. My father fought to have me present at the meetings. Standing against those who tried to keep the Templars a sausage fest.

He taught me how to fight and took me demon hunting from an early age. Turned out I was skilled at it, a good thing since I had to prove myself to the old-school knights who thought women belonged in the kitchen or in bed on their backs, legs spread. It took time and effort, but I finally reached a point in the organization where I demanded and received respect.

My induction was just the start. At the last major Templar event—a convention held in Italy that gathered all 304 knights scattered around the world—I'd been pleased to see how many female members now belonged to the various Templar cells. In an even more astonishing stroke, when my dad died unexpectedly last year from a heart attack, my own sect voted me in to replace him. Me, the nonreligious but willing-to-fight evil chick, now in charge of the group that the world assumed LARPed at being heroes. Little did they know, we did actually fight monsters; we just didn't advertise it.

Anyhow back to the angel. Given my shit day, I'd chosen to bunk down in the church basement with a bottle of Jack Daniel's—the only best friend a girl really had until the spins hit. I wasn't what you'd call the sociable type. Me and other girls? We didn't get along. I'd always understood guys so much better. Problem being, at one point, guy friends made a move that led to you having to not so gently rebuff them. I hated it when that happened. It spelled an end to hanging out because things always got awkward after the rejection.

Currently, I was taking a break from people because they tired me. Non-Templars didn't understand the secrets I kept. Templars wouldn't respect a leader fucking their members. It left me with few choices when it came to friendships. Thankfully Jack, that dear old bottle of soothing warmth, gave me exactly what I needed. Relaxation.

Since I didn't have a bed, I lay atop the table where I'd spread my blanket and pillow, some of the few things I'd managed to grab before being ushered out. Since the ceiling insisted on spinning, I had my eyes closed, one leg flopped over the side of the table, my toes dangling but not quite reaching the floor to steady me. I really hoped I could avoid puking. I'd forgotten to grab an elastic for my hair.

Bang. Bang. Bang. I was startled at the brisk knock at the side door, situated in the alley and giving direct access into the basement so you could avoid the church overhead. At the Templar meetings, we often joked about our underground meeting room being our version of a lair, hidden and secret. The irony being the church rented it to us thinking we were an anonymous addiction group. They ignored the odd hours we sometimes met. In return, we kept pesky demons out of the belfry and did it so well that the pastor and his many volunteers never saw a thing.

Given this wasn't a meeting night—I should know, I'm the one who calls them—I ignored the tap. If this were a Templar emergency—AKA demon sighting—they would have used the secret knock or, most likely given we'd gone modern at my urging, texted.

The person in the alley didn't bang a second time, and I expelled a breath as I opened my eyes. The view proved disconcerting seeing as how I'd left a light on. The covered windows made this place too dark and creepy otherwise. It didn't help it could have used a renovation starting with the ceiling. I stared at the drop tiles, more dingy gray than white, many of which sported yellow circles of mouse pee.

Click.

My half-lidded eyes flew open. I turned my head to see the knob on the door turning. Holy shit. Someone was coming inside.

I was understandably perturbed seeing as how only two other people had a key. Tony, who'd been trying to convince us to switch to Zoom permanently after Covid, seeing as he owned a super nice house in the burbs and hated coming to meetings. And Antonia, who currently vacationed in the Bahamas.

Despite the spinning of my brain, I rolled to my side and shoved my other leg off the table. Unfortunately, my body began to follow. My feet hit, and I crumpled, hitting the floor as the door opened. My hands barely stopped my fall. My nose almost kissed the tile floor. Hair flopped over my cheeks to form a veil, blocking my view. Worst of all, my gun was in my duffel bag on a chair opposite me.

Over the thumping of my heart, I heard a strange rustling and almost a scraping as if something shoved its way through the doorframe. Something big. Like a demon!

Shit. I went to push myself up, only to get the spins and a lurch in my tummy that didn't bode well. I paused and took a deep breath.

Thump, thump, thump. Steps approached. From a

tiny part in my hair, I noted the boots that stopped not far from my face. I hotly blew on a hank of hair —*Pfffft*—that did nothing to improve my line of sight.

"Are you injured?" asked a deep male voice with a gravelly undertone.

"Nope, just a little bit tipsy," I slurred as I shoved to my hands and knees, head still hanging. Ugh, why did gravity have to be such a jerk? I managed to get upright but only because a firm grip steadied me enough that I could lift my face and gape for a few reasons.

One, what a pretty man. You know that term "cheekbones sharp enough to cut"? I stared at them framed by the kind of layered hair men usually paid a fortune to achieve. A stern gaze met mine, which matched the thinly pressed lips. But what caused me to blink? The jutting wings at the intruder's back. Had to be a costume. A good one, too, given I'd have sworn I saw the feathers on them ruffle.

"Who are you?" I managed to ask despite my thick tongue.

"Metatron."

"Sounds like a good name for a Transformer. Only, usually, they don't have wings." My reply drew his brows together.

"I don't know what this transformer is that you speak of. I am an archangel here on a mission from God."

I'm afraid I laughed. "Sure you are, buddy." Because the thing was, yes, as a Templar Knight, I fought the forces of evil, AKA nuisance demons that popped up every so often, but while my order might be based on religion and, supposedly, we followed the word of God, I actually didn't really believe in it. I mean, if angels were real, why hadn't I ever seen any? I'd encountered enough demons to satisfy me they existed, but no burning bushes, no celestial beings, no voices out of nowhere, until now. And given my level of drunkenness, there existed a strong possibility the man cosplaying wasn't real. Never mind the fact I'd never hallucinated before. There was always a first time.

"You are alone?" he asked, glancing around.

The question managed a cold slap to my drunken fuzz. I stepped away from the guy called Metatron, and my back hit the table, preventing me from moving farther and still too far from my gun. With my tipsy state, what were the chances I could throw myself over the table, grab it from my bag and aim it—without falling over or puking?

Probably not good odds, so I remained still and cautious. Curious too. As some of my senses returned, I noted, despite his claim, the wings at his back weren't white but a strange teal. So, not an angel. At the same time, he wasn't like any demon I'd ever seen. He didn't have horns or any of the disfiguration I'd become used to. Twisted limbs, leathery appearance, and slavering grunts tended to be the norm.

"Listen, I don't know who you are, or how you got a key, but I know for a fact you shouldn't be here and need to leave." Had I been sober, I wouldn't have been so worried. I'd faced down monsters, gone and cleared out nests when they cropped up, and put myself numerous times in danger with the scars to prove it. But I knew my instincts were off. Hand-to-hand against a guy his size would be tricky if I couldn't count on my usual speed.

I inched sideways, keeping my eyes on him as I made my way to my bag.

"I came because your door bore the symbol." To my surprise, he sketched the Templar sign in the air, a cross that then lit up bright red before fading from sight.

Okay, that was kind of cool and more proof I probably dreamed this. "What do you want with the Templars?"

"You know of them?" he countered.

No point in lying given the symbol lightly etched on the top left corner of the door. "Yeah, I know of them."

"Where can I find their leader?"

"Depends on why you want them." I cocked my head. "How did you even find this location?" It wasn't as if we advertised our presence.

"The sign—"

"On the door is tiny and barely noticeable. In other words, unless you know where to find it, it's not something you just come across," I countered. "So let's try again. Why did you come to this church in particular?" It was one of dozens in the city, but the only Templar one in the state.

"It wasn't the symbol on your door that alerted me to your presence but the design on the roof."

My turn to purse my lips. "What design?"

Once more he did a sketch in the air, the cross somehow having ornate flairs to the ends, the red of it more muted, a burgundy to match the clay tile used on the roof. The symbol faded. "I happened to be flying overhead when I saw it. I'd begun to think the previous choir failed to establish the Templars or that they'd disappeared along with the shepherds."

"The Templars are still around, but the only shepherds in this world usually tend to sheep."

"How many knights serve?" he asked.

"Why does it matter?"

"Because this planet is in grave danger."

A grand declaration. I crossed my arms. "Oh. From what, pray tell?"

"Hell."

Maybe it was because I remained drunk, but I laughed. "Of course it has to be Hell. Nice." I clapped. "You are good. I mean the wings, the earnest expressions. Who put you up to this? Was it Edward? Or Leopold? Is there a camera taping this?"

I glanced around, looking for a hidden lens or person holding up a phone.

"Woman, you are testing my patience. I do not have time for your mockery. Where is the Templar leader? I need to speak with him at once."

No surprise he'd assume a male was in charge. It soured my mirth. "Listen, pal. Fun's over. You and your fake-ass wings need to go before I call the cops." Or shot him. The more the alcoholic buzz wore off, the more my trigger finger itched. If this guy wasn't cosplaying, then I faced a next-level demon.

He drew himself straighter, which made his already impressive height daunting. His eyes began to glow but not as much as the halo that suddenly circled his head, and when he spoke again, his voice reverberated. "Enough of your blathering, woman. Take me to the Templar leader at once!" His wings extended, and I still couldn't help myself.

"You can take your demands and shove them, demon."

He uttered a sound as he reached for me, but I darted away, or meant to. My drunken butt lacked coordination, meaning he managed to grab hold of my arm and swing me back to face him.

He uttered a growly noise I didn't understand. His halo brightened, and through the still-open door, a light beamed and bathed us in its brilliance.

I blinked, and when I could see again, we

weren't in that church basement anymore. A disjointed sensation hit me hard. My stomach heaved. And by heaved, I mean it decided to evacuate through my mouth.

And that was how I barfed all over my first angel.

CHAPTER 2

Metatron held on to his annoyance lest he smite the human who'd fouled all over him. Frustrating creature that she was, he should have probably left her when she proved so contrary. However, seeing the Templar symbol when flying overhead, the sigil used to identify those doing work for the shepherds guiding the flock, excited him. Perhaps this planet hadn't forgotten everything if the Templars still existed. They could be of great aid in navigating this strange planet.

Having visited many flocks in his life, he'd never met one that had evolved in such a fashion. Blame the fact they'd lost their shepherds—AKA the ark and angels sent to guide them.

He whirled from the woman who stared around wide-eyed and non-apologetic about the mess she'd made. He stalked a few paces before spreading his arms and commanding the cantorii to cleanse him. It removed the vile fluids and chunks from him but could do nothing for his mood. That remained dark.

To think he'd been banished to this.

"I don't feel so good," she slurred.

He whirled to see the human had collapsed on his narrow bed. He didn't use it often, preferring to perch when he slept. While only slightly wider than his frame, it should have been big enough for the slight female if she'd used it properly, but she lay sprawled at an angle that dangled her head over one edge and legs over another while she snored something terrible.

He pursed his lips. She wasn't ill, but drunk, which God condemned along with the use of drugs and other debaucheries.

Not that Elyon abstained. Metatron might not have partaken, but he was aware of Elyon's vices, usually hidden from all but those closest to him. *Do as I say, not as I do,* what Elyon had once declared when Metatron had dared to question God about his choices.

Metatron poked at the female. "Wake up."

Snort. Snuffle. The woman didn't rouse.

He sighed; he didn't have time for this. He contacted Jesus, God's scion—and spy. Each cantorii and ark travelled with one, an extension of Elyon himself, a Jesus who had some of God's powers, enough to keep a mission healthy and impress the flocks on the colonized planets. Most were annoying and pompous with an inflated sense of worth despite being the lowest ranked when on a mission. This Jesus in particular irritated Metatron to the point he'd thought about having him expelled into space.

"*What?*" Jesus replied via the HALO.

Metatron fought the urge to snap. The constant disrespect grated. Not to mention this particular Jesus Christ's reputation proceeded him. Angels had a tendency of dying on missions with this one. It led to Metatron taking a few precautions to ensure he didn't also become a casualty.

"*I have a human in need of healing,*" Metatron explained.

"*Why not just kill it and grab another? There's billions of them on this filthy planet.*" The biggest colony Metatron had ever encountered and the one person he needed sleeping off their overindulgence.

"*Now.*" His final growled word on the matter.

Jesus chose to not further argue and appeared at the door to his room a short moment after. The male entered, his hair long and unruly, his frame gaunt, unlike the last Jesus Metatron worked with. This one had already adopted the clothing from the surface and could have fit right in with his sulky expression.

"What's wrong with her?" Jesus groused as he headed for the bed.

"Intoxication."

Jesus halted and whirled. "That's not an injury."

"She is incapacitated, and I need her coherent."

Jesus huffed. "How will she learn her lesson on over-imbibing if I heal her?"

Metatron simply stared. Long and hard.

Jesus sighed and sulked his way to the woman's side. He knelt and placed his hands on her. A glow immediately encased them both.

While Jesus worked, Metatron did a check-in via his HALO to see what had happened while he'd been out. The ship eagerly let him sift its surveillance records. There were times he thought he felt a glimmer of emotion. Could it be the cantorii peaked early and would soon be achieving ark sentience status? The floor vibrated under his feet as if the cantorii heard him and replied.

Jesus stated, "It's done. She should wake any moment."

"Thank you."

Jesus rose and tucked his hands into his pockets as he stared down at the woman. "Who is she?"

"Someone with information."

Jesus glanced at him. "You know I could have just rifled her memories to find it."

Rather than shudder in distaste at the offer to dig inside her mind—and leave it scrambled—Metatron dismissed Jesus. "I have the situation in wing. You can return to your previous activity."

Jesus cast one last glance at the woman before

slinking out. Metatron really should do something about God's scion before anything happened. Jesus might appear benign, but he had too much power—and a cruel streak.

The woman stirred, yawning and stretching, rolling to her back, her clothes filthy. He grimaced as he ordered the ship to cleanse her. It led to the female sitting suddenly upright, eyes wide, wiggling and shaking.

"Eep. What's that tickle? Stop." She squirmed as the ship removed all traces of foulness from her skin and clothes. When it finished, and she stopped jiggling, she looked around, taking a moment to notice her surroundings. Craning her head, she passed a glance over him a few times before narrowing her gaze.

"Where am I?"

"My room."

"You fucking kidnapped me!" she yelled, rising from the bed.

"You refused to give me the information I requested."

She advanced on him, cheeks bright with fury, matching her sparking gaze. He'd not noticed before the beauty she presented. Now alert, her expression fierce, he couldn't help but see not only her striking features framed by dark hair but her shapely figure.

"You made a big mistake," she snarled as she neared enough to swing a fist.

He caught it, slightly surprised. In Elyon's army, only male angels ever fought. The rare females, wingless and beautiful, remained on Heaven. On Eden, a place the humans had renamed Earth, the two sexes comingled, the females in positions of power usually unheard of in most colonies. Very few ever established matriarchal dominance. None ever showed such parity of position like Earth.

A foot followed the fist and hit him in the ribs. He could have shielded but didn't. Instead, he blocked her blows, his bracers harder than her little fists.

Soon she blew hotly and glared but, recognizing she wouldn't prevail, showed intelligence at last and held her hands by her sides.

"Done?" he asked.

"Only until I find something sharp."

Her threat rolled right off his wingtip. "Now that you are coherent, you will tell me where to find the Templar leader. I need to speak with him at once."

"Why?" she countered.

"It is a matter of urgency."

She stared.

She must be simple-minded, as he'd told her earlier. "Hell is coming."

"Some would say it's already here." She moved from him and went to inspect the walls, running her hands over them.

"Not yet, but it's approaching. I fear this planet has little time."

"Little time for what?"

"To attempt evacuation and mount a defense."

She paused and half turned. "A defense against an attack? From whom? And don't say Hell again. I want an actual country or organization."

"I am tired of explaining to you, woman. I need the Templar leader. He'll understand what I'm speaking of."

"Oh really?" she drawled. "Is that because he's a man?"

"Because he will be versed in the Templar role as protectors against Hell."

"They don't need you to tell them how to do their job. Templars have already been protecting the world for thousands of years. Without them, we'd live in a much more demon-infested place."

"Minor skirmishes compared to what is coming. If Hell makes it to your planet, they will strip it of everything and kill almost everyone."

"You really should get some ominous music to go with that threat." She tapped the wall, walked a few paces, tapped again.

"I am very much regretting having you healed," he grumbled. Maybe she required a little suffering to humble her haughty attitude.

"Oh, so now you perform miracles too?" she taunted.

"I wasn't the one to heal you. That would be Jesus."

"Of course," she snorted. "Who else would be hanging around a supposed angel?"

"I'M NOT A SUPPOSED ANYTHING. I am an archangel in Elyon's army of light."

"And I'm the queen of Candy Land. What are you really? Demon? Something else?"

"How can you not believe I'm an angel?" It baffled him.

"Your wings are blue."

"And?"

"Angel's wings are white, duh." She rolled her eyes. "And you're like wearing dark clothing, very much not soldier of light."

"The white uniform is only for ceremonial events, and I don't understand what my appearance has to do with me being an archangel."

"Oh stop it already. Angels aren't real," she blurted out.

"You are standing in front of one," his dry reply.

"All right then, prove it." A request he'd never before encountered. It left him at a loss.

"How?"

"Let me meet God."

"God's on Heaven."

"Duh. Take me there to meet him and I'll believe you're an angel."

"Heaven's not close enough for us to beam."

"Is that some weird way of saying I'm too alive to visit? Because if so, that's a good thing. I kind of worried I was dead seeing as how this room doesn't have a door, or windows for that matter."

"Are you always this contrary?" he countered.

"I should have known you'd be the type who can't stand a woman who can speak her mind."

"I'd like it better if you spoke of the Templar leader's location."

"Right in front of you."

He frowned. "What's that supposed to mean? How is that an address?"

"No address needed because you're talking to her. Yes, a dumb woman is the one in charge of your precious Templars."

"You?" He stared at her in shock.

"Yes me."

He shook his head in disbelief. "If you're what the Templars have to offer, then I fear your world is doomed."

CHAPTER 3

Metatron's comment about the world being doomed would have gotten him gutted if I had a knife. I took offense at his disdain for me, especially because he based it solely on the fact I didn't have a sausage between my legs.

At the same time, I'd not given him any reason to respect me, given I A) had been stupidly drunk, B) puked on him, and C) called him a liar this entire time. Time to stop being a stubborn idiot. Time to stop denying I argued with a living breathing man with wings and a halo. Let's also not forget his ability to not only move me places but heal me. I'd never felt this good. Energized, awake, and alive in a way that convinced me more than anything that Metatron was an angel whom I'd royally insulted and pissed off.

And what did I do to improve his perception of

me? Retorted with a sarcastic, "Behold the sexist angel here to put me in my place."

"I don't know what this word sexist means."

"It means you have no respect for women and our abilities. We're not just baby-making machines, you know."

"Perhaps that is true on your planet. However, in most colonies, and even places outside the purview of Heaven, societies tend to run toward the masculine when it comes to ruling, the exception being the hives in the forbidden Manta Galaxy ruled by queens and princesses."

So much to unpack in that one sentence. I shook my head. "Well, on Earth, girls are now considered on par with boys, so you're gonna have to deal with it, Tron."

He frowned. "My name is Metatron."

"Which is a serious mouthful that makes me want to yell *Transformers, robots in disguise*." He stared at me blankly, and I shook my head. "You obviously aren't from around here."

"I'm from a galaxy far away."

I snickered. "This just keeps getting better and better, Tron."

His lips pressed into a line. "Call me as you wish, woman. I care not."

"Do not call me *woman*. My name is Francesca."

"Very well, Francesca, leader of the Templars. I am here on behalf of God and Heaven. Your world is in grave danger. Will you answer the call to fight?"

My lips parted because the damned man glowed when he said it; his halo, his body, and most especially his eyes. I almost reached out, curious and wondering in that moment if I'd burn at the touch, but he awaited my answer.

"Before I agree to anything, I want to know more about you, and this..." I waved to the room, and as my hand passed in front of my face, I noticed something. I paused and brought my hand to my face. Where had my scar gone? I'd had it for years on the base of my thumb from when I'd dumbly burned it sliding something out of the oven. The stark white knot had disappeared; my flesh appeared blemish free.

He saw me staring and offered an explanation. "Jesus healed you."

I blinked. "Excuse me?"

"You were incapacitated, and since I needed to speak with you, I had the Jesus on board the cantorii heal you."

"As in the actual Jesus Christ? Son of God?" I gaped.

"Scion, not son," he corrected.

"What's the difference?"

"A son is born of whereas a scion is a living extension of."

Whatever. I'd missed an introduction to Jesus

Christ because I'd been passed out drunk. "Can I meet him?"

"No."

"Why not? How do I know Jesus Christ actually healed me?"

The angel sighed and waved his hand. An image appeared of the room we stood in and me, passed out on a bed, not looking so hot. No wonder he remained unimpressed with me. I watched as a hippy dude who could have played Shaggy entered, put his hands over me, glowed, and voila, I roused, healed of every ache and pain.

"Wow." I couldn't help but be impressed.

Tron appeared impatient. "Satisfied now?"

No, but I was working on it. "Where are we?"

"Aboard the cantorii, which is currently orbiting your planet."

I snorted. "I think I would have heard if there was a spaceship spying on Earth."

"We're cloaked."

"Of course you are." The hits to my reality kept coming. Cloaking was something you heard about in sci-fi adventures but didn't actually exist yet outside of movies. "And let me guess. We beamed here." I did remember a bright light.

"Yes. Are we done with your mundane questions?" a terse query.

"Not entirely. I want to clarify something. You

say you're an angel employed by God, who lives in Heaven—"

"Hallowed be his name," he offered quite seriously.

It threw me for a second. "And you're here because..."

"My choir was sent on a mission of exploration. We discovered your lost colony by chance and have been ordered to retrieve as much suul as we can."

"What's s-o-o-l?" I tried to repeat it with his inflection.

"What's left behind when one of the flock dies."

I blinked. "You're stealing souls?"

He frowned. "Hardly theft. Your planet is teeming with suul. We are simply harvesting it."

"You're slaughtering us for our souls?" I screeched.

"No!" he snapped. "We simply gather what's already there from those who've passed."

"And where does Hell fit into all this?"

"Hell has become aware of your planet's existence and is coming to strip it of its resources."

"Like you."

"Hardly."

"You just said you were going to *harvest* souls." Stated with finger quotes.

"What we do won't harm the planet, unlike Hell, which will literally take everything; mineral, animal, water."

"In other words, they want to start the apocalypse, which is why you've come seeking Templars because you need us to fight the forces of evil."

"Actually, we'll need to recruit as much of humanity as possible to fight back. Although, ideally, your planet will have the means to nullify the risk before Hell arrives."

"Where is it supposed to show up? Is Hell tunneling its way up in only one area or many?" I imagined a machine boring through the earth to the surface, releasing a torrent of fiery demons.

"Hell will be in the spiral arm of your galaxy shortly. Soon, it will be visible by your telescopes."

"Wait, Hell is an asteroid?" Duh, kind of made sense if Heaven was in space. Still... super unexpected at the same time.

"Perhaps, at one time, it began as a rock, but over time, it has evolved into something much larger than that. The more planets it devours, the more immense it becomes, making it ponderous but mighty."

"Damn, that's a lot to take in," I muttered, planting my hands on my hips and chewing my lower lip. "Guess I'd better start brushing up on my Bible passages, which appear to have left quite a few bits out. Like the fact angels came from space. Are you an alien?" Would he smite me for asking? Guess we'd find out.

His lips twisted. "By your world's definition, yes."

"But you're also known as angels because you've been here before. People remembered you and gave your kind a name."

"They didn't give it to us," he replied, his tone frosty. "We've always been angels."

Testy, testy. I continued with my questions. After all, my agnostic side demanded it. "I've seen the pictures. God's angels have white wings. Those who've fallen are usually gray or black. I've never heard or seen them teal-colored."

Disdain curled his mouth. "Ah yes, because humanity all share the same color of skin and hair."

I pursed my lips at his rebuke even as I continued questioning. "You said Heaven isn't nearby. If that's the case, how do souls get to it when they die?"

"They haven't. Not yet at any rate. Somehow after the seeding, your planet got forgotten, its shepherds lost. Given the number of disciples who died, the suul has accumulated so much it made Eden the most valuable deposit I've ever seen."

"In other words, Earth is swimming in the souls of dead people." My nose wrinkled. "Kind of gross."

"Suul is a valuable resource used by God for creation."

His choice of words struck me. "As in an actual god who makes stuff?"

"Do you repeat everything people say?"

I'd never wanted to slap someone more. "I'm going to guess that the moment you realized we were a fountain of souls you notified this god."

"It is my duty to report at regular intervals and if we come across anything of interest. A lost flock would count."

His choice of words caused me to bristle. "We are not sheep."

"The correct term is disciples."

"But not everyone believes in your god. Some worship many."

"There is only one. How can you be a Templar and not know that?" he accused, and I had to admit, "I never really believed in the religion part of being a knight. I am dedicated to making sure the monsters can't hurt anyone."

"At least at your core, your cause remains noble, making you suitable for the task ahead." A begrudging admission.

"What exactly do you want of the Templars?"

"We need to marshal your forces and plan a defense. Your technology is advanced enough you might be able to repel the impending attack."

"Against an asteroid?" I couldn't help an incredulous note. "We're knights who fight on the earth, not up in the sky. You'll want astronauts for that." Only in the movies did Earth have space marines and starship troopers.

His brows drew close. "Are astronauts a branch of the Templar?"

"No. Do you not know anything of Earth at all?"

"We are only recently arrived, and I was busy trying to avert Hell's attention, to no avail as it turned out."

"Might I suggest you get caught up on a bit of our modern history?"

"I don't need to. It became quickly obvious your kind is good at waging war and causing destruction. Exactly what is needed if you're to survive the impending attack."

"Let me guess, angels are all peace and love," I stated, and yet eyeing him, he appeared nothing like it. For one, the big-ass sword strapped to his hip indicated otherwise.

"Only those who live upon Heaven enjoy a life free of strife. It is up to Elyon's Warriors to protect and enforce God's laws so that nothing impinges on their happiness and safety."

"Meaning even in Heaven there are different classes. Are there angels lower on the ladder than soldiers?"

His lips pursed. "Whatever role God assigns us is a privilege."

"If you say so." I waved a hand. "I don't suppose you have any books I can read. You know like history texts, maybe some magazines or newspapers. Videos are good too."

He pursed his lips. "We do not use those methods of information collection. Too prone to destruction."

"Then how do you pass on history and knowledge?"

He tapped his temple. "Active HALOs record and that information ends up stored on Heaven."

"But it's obviously not fool proof. You said you lost Earth and just found it again."

His lips went into a tight line. "Heaven hasn't been without strife. We didn't realize at the time the extent of the damage."

"Let me guess, Heaven got in a fight with Hell."

"Actually, we were allies in that skirmish against a more dire threat."

"Must have been bad if you guys joined sides." Glad it never came here. "If Hell is flying here, does that mean Heaven's coming, too, to help us?"

He shrugged. "Maybe. No one knows what Elyon will do."

"Who's Elyon?"

"God."

"He has a name?"

"Why wouldn't he?"

He? Why was I not surprised?

"Will you help?" Tron repeated.

"I am not going to be kidnapped and coerced into something without knowing more first." On this I wouldn't budge.

"Very well. The cantorii will show you. I will speak to you when you're done."

With that, he left, and I might have lost my shot, only the room suddenly turned into a giant video. It showed me a massive shape coming into view of a planet, the underside of it a series of fluted holes. From them emerged demons. Hundreds of them, but not the ugly ones seen on Earth. Men and women, muscled and clad in armor, bearing swords as well as guns, flew on dark leathery wings. Some wore helms, and those with horns had them growing back over their skulls. A few had nubs, as if they'd been sheared. They descended upon a planet with swaying yellow stalks under an intense violet sky.

There were people on the ground but not entirely human. They had two arms and legs, eyes and a mouth, even hair and fingers that could grasp their farming tools. But their skin was olive green, and their lack of noses and their tails were very much alien.

Some ran in panic. Others watched as the demons swooped, some of them to steal those fleeing. Swords scythed into the few who dared to wave a makeshift weapon.

The capture of the village took minutes, the people rounded up, even the little ones. A demon walked among those kneeling and pulled some out at random, sending them sobbing to a cage lowered from the ship.

The chosen were taken away, and the demons soon followed. Not long after, the suction began, the funnels in the bottom of the ship sucking and pulling, drawing up everything on the surface, plant, animal, those left behind. By the time the ship finished its pillaging, only a bare rock remained.

Horrifying if true. And the menace was coming here to do the same to Earth.

When Metatron returned, I gave him my answer. "How can the Templars help?"

CHAPTER 4

FRANCESCA FINALLY AGREED TO PLEDGE THE TEMPLARS TO help, which should have been automatic, but anyhow. Rather than be done with the interrogation, Metatron then got stuck with a litany of questions.

"*How long until the threat arrives? What kind of defense do they have? How do we fight against flying demons? What kind of weapons will they wield?*"

Then she had the ones he had no replies for. "*Have you contacted the various governments to enlist their aid? Are you aware of how many missiles we can launch? Where do you think Hell will launch its army first?*"

Only the last question did he have an answer for. "*What kind of offense system does your spaceship have?*" None. Because God wouldn't allow it.

She'd eyed him and whistled. *"Wow must suck to know you're expendable."*

The comment stung because it was true. Metatron knew of angels on board who would have argued God loved them. He knew better. Elyon had stopped caring about those he governed. Metatron just couldn't figure out exactly when it happened or why.

Given Francesca made him uncomfortable, not just with her pointed truths but her actual presence—causing a surge of lust he'd long thought over and done with—he avoided her as much as possible. He set her back in that horrible room underground and offered her a token she could use to contact him. But he did warn, *"Use it sparingly as it might attract unwanted attention."*

She didn't use it at all the first day. The second, he kept having the cantorii peek in on her, zeroing in on her location because she at least had the good sense to keep his tracking device with her. He just couldn't actually see inside the basement where she resided. No windows to peek through and a door that she kept shut. The only time it opened? When she allowed people entry, mostly males, who arrived at the door marked with the Templar symbol and knocked in the same pattern each time.

Only once did she depart, and Metatron found himself distracted keeping track of her as she walked rapidly to a different set of stairs that descended into the ground. She used what the humans called a subway to travel. The cantorii lost her until she emerged from the underground and entered a shop. She eventually left with an armful of books that appeared quite heavy. He almost swooped in to give her a hand because he'd not been able to help himself from beaming close by. He'd done so above the clouds to avoid being seen and draped himself in an invisibility cloak that he might better skulk atop a rooftop.

What did she want with the heavy tomes? He couldn't see their titles, but she apparently valued them enough that she hailed a conveyance marked "Taxi" and used it to return to the church basement. A church that Elyon would be displeased with, given its previous grandeur had faded.

Not humanity's fault. Once the choir sent to Eden failed to keep the flock in order, they would have had no one left to guide them. According to Elyon, who'd been the one to identify the lost colony as Eden, its shepherd, Noah, had only himself to blame. By not culling as Elyon commanded, he allowed the humans autonomy, which led to them eventually killing off the choir, including Jesus Christ.

Unheard of, and yet, because of their actions, the colony formerly known as Eden might just have what it took to repel Hell, perhaps even become a sovereign power of its own, but only with some help. Help that Metatron meted out cautiously. After all, humanity appeared to have eliminated the last choir that got involved with their affairs.

A second day passed with Francesca not contacting him. She left the basement only once to fetch some food. The fleeting glimpse proved a temptation, and an annoyance. Why hadn't she reached out? Surely by now she had more annoying questions.

When night fell, Metatron couldn't help but return to pay her a visit. This time he knew the proper tapping sequence. When she opened the door, her lips curved in a smile. "I wondered when you'd be back. We have much to talk about."

"You didn't contact me." He failed to completely erase the whine from the statement.

She shrugged. "I figured you'd come around again." Meaning she'd been playing a game of waiting—and won.

It led to him being stiff in his reply. "How goes the preparation with the knights? Are they readying for war?"

"Not exactly." She ushered him inside and shut the door before adding, "Remember how I was skeptical about you?"

"You accused me of being a demon." His lip curled at the reminder.

"With good reason, given what I've been taught. And this goes to the point that it took me a bit to believe you actually were who you claimed. I've been telling my sect about you, and Hell and everything, but..." She rolled her shoulders. "A few of them think I need to see a doctor seeing as how I'm talking about alien angels. Can't say as I blame them. It's a hard sell trying to convince the knights we need to get ready for a war with a space demon when there's nothing in the sky yet."

"They require proof." Irritating, but easily rectified. "What do you suggest?"

Her finger pointed in his direction. "Using you. Everyone needs to meet you and see that you're real. Once we get past that part, we show them some of those Hell videos I saw on your spaceship."

He couldn't help but grimace. "You wish me to parade myself. Can we not simply show them holograms?"

"With today's CGI, a video would be debunked as fake. We need you in the flesh, where my people can interact and see for themselves you exist."

He couldn't help a rebuke. "It is very inconvenient that your planet has chosen to forget who and what we are."

"Get over it." She waved him off. "You're the one who came to me for help, and I'm telling you what has to be done. So will you stick around so I can call an emergency meeting?"

A forbearing sigh slipped from Metatron. "If I must."

The moment he agreed, Francesca became a whirlwind of activity, her fingers flying on her phone, answering calls, and even setting up a laptop.

It wasn't long before people began to arrive, straggling in singly or a pair at a time. Not even close to an army, which he'd already suspected given the size of their headquarters.

Eyes kept straying to him, and he heard the whispers. *"Demon? Gargoyle? What's going on?"*

Not one of them said angel. He could only assume it had to do with the ridiculous wing theory, as if white were the only acceptable shade. Valor and skill were what mattered.

By the time the thirteenth person entered, Francesca clapped her hands and the room quieted. "Thank you for coming on short notice."

"Message said it was important." The speaker's gaze strayed to Metatron.

"It is, Maury, but before we get started, Simon, pull down the screen please."

A male rose to tug on a ring, which caused a white panel to descend. Francesca typed on her laptop and another device shot out a beam of light that hit the screen and then split into several boxes, each holding a face.

Curious despite himself, Metatron kept silent and listened.

"Evening, fellow Templars. My sect here knows

me, but for those who manage to join us via Zoom, I'm Francesca Moretti, head of the Pittsburgh Chapter. And I'm here to introduce you to someone with an important message." She turned and gestured to Metatron.

Time to put himself on display. Metatron held in a sigh as he joined her. There were gasps. Mostly from those projected on the screen.

"What are you doing with a demon?" hissed a portly male in the bottom corner.

"Not a demon, Clemons, he's an angel," she corrected. "Simon, can you video from different angles so they can see his wings are real." A fellow with short blond hair approached with his phone, and Metatron resisted an urge to slap it out of his hand. He hated the theatrics of proving himself. It should have been obvious. His wings flared and ruffled as Simon neared. There were more audible exclamations, as he also ignited his HALO and growled.

"I am Metatron, archangel in Elyon's Army of Light, principality of the cantorii and, given your missing shepherd and his choir, currently the one in charge of Eden's flock."

At his announcement, silence reigned for a moment before someone whispered, "Is he calling us sheep?"

Then a cacophony broke out, as voices shouted in person and on the screen, too many at once.

"Silence!" Metatron boomed, and his HALO flared bright, outlining him in golden light. "The Templars are sworn to God's service, and I am now calling on that vow to ready yourself to fight, for Hell is coming."

Laughter broke out and a derisive, "Ooh, the devil's going to do what? Set the world on fire?"

"Behold!" Metatron gave the order to his HALO, and he showed them the destruction of a planet.

To which the same nonbeliever retorted, "Nice special effects."

Metatron stared him down, but the bold fellow held his gaze. He managed to ask through a gritted jaw, "Your name."

The brash one stood. "Cain."

"That scar on your face, why have you not had it healed?" Metatron had taken note that the rest of the young male appeared fit.

Cain's lips twisted. "Because I can't afford the surgery. Thanks for pointing it out, asshole."

"So you would remove it if you could?" Metatron queried.

"Well, yeah."

Metatron held up his hand and sent a command to the cantorii. Not long after, Jesus Christ walked through the door. Literally. One of his scion powers included the ability to temporarily suspend his physical presence. A person in the back row noticed his entrance and gasped, leading to some heads turning and more whispers. *"Who is that? Who let him in?"*

Soon all the people in the room were fidgeting and watching as Jesus joined Metatron and Francesca at the top of the room.

Metatron held up his hand. "Behold, God's scion, Jesus Christ."

He didn't expect the wave of laughter that followed and blamed Jesus. His choice to wear human garments meant he didn't appear very Heavenly.

Jesus didn't appear happy with the response to his name and scowled. "Shall I smite them for their disrespect?"

"No. We need the knights. But it appears they require proof we are who we say." Metatron pointed to Cain. "Heal that man." He then jabbed his finger at Simon. "You will video it so the others can see."

Jesus sauntered to Cain, who remained sneering with his arms crossed. "Lucky me. Jesus Christ himself is gonna lay his hands on me. Praise be."

"It is not I you should praise, but God, for I am merely his vessel." Jesus floated off the floor, and a glow circled him as he stretched out his hands.

The amount of murmurs that erupted held more reverence than Metatron would have expected.

"How can you be Jesus Christ? The Bible says he died for our sins," Maury stated.

"God has many scions, and I have been sent here

to bring you back into his fold." For once, Jesus looked loving. It helped he had the rapt attention of the assembled knights.

"How do we know you're telling the truth?" Cain blustered. "Maybe you're just good at doing tricks."

"Behold the power of God!" Jesus clapped his hands, and thunder erupted, along with a bright flash of light. He held out his glowing hands, close to but not touching Cain. He didn't need contact to heal.

The holy spirit contained within Jesus emerged to bath Cain in its brilliance. When it extinguished, the knotted and red scar on the man's face had disappeared.

It led to much yelling and pleading as others asked if Jesus could fix them too.

"First, let us give thanks." Jesus bowed his head, "Our God, who are upon Heaven, hallowed be thy name…"

As those assembled joined in the prayer, Francesca sidled close. "Good thinking calling JC in to convince them. I was beginning to think they were going to vote to stab you in case you actually were a demon."

"They would have tried," his dry reply.

"I don't think you'll have a problem convincing them now."

His lip curled. "Doubtful. Humanity seems plagued with questions."

"Curiosity is not a crime."

"It is when it delays action."

"Well, they're listening now," she remarked, given the group crowded around Jesus as he healed the next person.

"I supposed that's all that matters. Given we've accomplished our goal of making them believe, I'll leave you to finish the meeting."

"Wait, you're leaving?"

"I have other matters to attend," he stated as he strode for the door. He exited to find Francesca on his heels.

"You can't just go," she huffed.

"Why not? My presence isn't needed. Jesus can answer anything you need to know."

"I thought you were in charge."

"I am. However, it seems he is better suited for the theatric displays. When it comes to actual planning of combat situations, then I will be more involved." The basement door closed behind them.

He'd extinguished his HALO before stepping outside, and the dim alley didn't provide much illumination to see her expression.

"I hope by 'involved' you mean you're planning to teach us some strategy, because I'm going to be honest with you. I've only ever been involved in small operations. None of us have ever been in a full-scale war."

"Everyone has a first time." He still remembered

his. An established and popular colony on a beautiful planet used by the angels on Heaven as a vacation location. So many of them chose to remain that Mesopotamia became known as the second Heaven, until roving space pirates found it.

When the invasion occurred, Metatron had only recently left the creche and been elevated to his position. His first mission dropped him in the thick of the conflict, a violent chaos that frightened. He remembered his wide-eyed panic at the bodies on the ground, dead and bleeding, the pirates, looking savage with their tusks and scimitars, covered in gore barreling for him. Only his training saved his life.

His arm swept his blade in automatic defense, shearing through flesh then stabbing the pirate in the chest. He still remembered the surprised look in his opponent's eyes before life vacated the body.

That was only his first kill. By the time the conflict ended, the blood and guts of those he'd laid to permanent rest smothered his skin and caked his feathers.

"Where do I even start to prepare?" she asked.

"Firstly, I'd suggest finding a location that can assemble an army. Somewhere defensible and hidden, where the knights and new recruits can train out of sight of the enemy."

"A place like that might be hard to find in the

city," she mused aloud. "But I think I know just the place where we won't be disturbed."

"Along with a location, you'll want to muster weapons. Bladed is best for close fighting, but you'll also want long-range. And not just firearms. Crossbows and other missile types are recommended."

"You're kidding, right? Bows aren't something that can be quickly or easily learned, not to mention expensive to source."

"Slingshots can be effective with the right missile and, given the ease with which they can be made, a good alternative to outfit everyone with."

Her nose wrinkled. "A slingshot? Isn't that a kids' toy?"

He blinked at her. "You let your children play with them?"

"Slingshots aren't really considered weapons." She shrugged.

"And yet, fire a rock with one and it will tear through a wing, bringing imps and demons in reach." He pointed out the obvious before continuing. "You'll want to gather supplies of all types, food, clothing, anything needed to survive a siege. You'll want to have these stashed in numerous locations should one place be compromised."

"If the feds noticed us stockpiling guns and bombs, they'll start asking questions."

The term had him frowning. "Who are these feds?"

"Government officials. The kind of stuff you're asking for might trigger some alarms. What are we supposed to say if a terrorism task force comes poking?"

"Tell them the truth, that you are preparing to save Earth."

"Ah yes, because they'll totally believe me." She rolled her eyes. "You saw how hard they were to convince inside."

His lips pursed, but before he could reply, an imp plunged from the sky!

CHAPTER 5

NOTHING LIKE HAVING A SERIOUS DISCUSSION INTERRUPTED by a monster. It dropped from above, its wings tucked as it arrowed with claws out, all the while hissing through its fangs.

Tron didn't even flinch. Heck, I'd have sworn he knew it was coming the way he smoothly pulled his sword, the blade of it gleaming as it swung and sheared through the flying body. The demon hit the ground in two pieces, and I gaped. Tron showed impressively fast reflexes for a big guy.

He glanced overhead. "Give me a moment." He shot up into the sky, his wings furled at his back, and yet he managed to clear the roof line of not only the church but the three-story building alongside. A mighty leap that left me gaping.

I couldn't see much of what happened next, but judging by the screeches, demons died. When Metatron returned, he appeared uninjured and unruffled. Pun intended.

"How many were there?" I asked.

"Only a few but that's enough. Your location is compromised. You'll have to move," he noted.

"Hate to break it to you but the monsters have known we're here for a while, on purpose, I might add. We make them come to us since they're good at hiding. Since we started baiting, we usually dispatch three or four a month."

"Meaning they've yet to launch a large-scale attack," he stated as if it were just a matter of time. "You will have issues should they ever outnumber you."

"That would require them pre-planning, which they're not smart enough to do."

His lips pinched. "With Hell coming, things will change. You need to be ready."

"We've been doing just fine thus far."

"Fine isn't good enough. Those on the surface will be driven into a murderous frenzy as the Dark Lord of Hell nears."

"Why?" I couldn't help myself, and he sighed as his gaze went skyward.

"Because their simple minds will be overwhelmed with a need to please their master."

"And by pleasing you mean killing." I grimaced. "Lovely. Another thing to worry about. Anything else I should know? Like, is Hell going to cause dormant volcanoes to go haywire? Should I expect geostorms?"

Once more his expression pinched in disapproval. "You're mocking my warning."

"More like overwhelmed. This is a lot to take in. And every time I think I understand what's going on, you drop another bombshell."

"The best thing you can do is be prepared to fight, and soon, and to that end, you should return to the meeting. Make sure the Templars are readying themselves."

"Easier said than done," I muttered. People-wrangling wasn't easy. Managing personalities required a fine balancing act. About the only time they didn't squabble was when we actually had something to fight.

"If you require me, you have the token to contact."

My hand dropped to my pocket at the reminder even as I blinked, the bright light that encased him too much for my poor eyes.

When I could see again, he'd disappeared. Beamed back to his ship. Leaving me with a monumental task; wrangling the Templars into an army to fight Hell while, at the same time, recruiting and outfitting because from what I'd seen in the historic footage of previous Hell invasions, a few hundred knights wouldn't be enough.

The meeting where I introduced Metatron and

Jesus Christ got the ball rolling with my sect and those present via webcam. They pledged their support, but I knew this was just the beginning. We had much work to do and questions to answer.

While most would be content to follow and do whatever Jesus or the angels said, I dug deeper, wanting to understand more about the mysterious visitors from outer space. I immersed myself in learning whatever I could about the angels, Hell, Heaven, and the God called Elyon. It turned out I didn't need Tron around to answer my questions because I somehow befriended his ship, who turned out to be an intelligent living being who called herself Zilla. I was just as surprised the first time I heard her voice. Apparently, the angels on board couldn't hear her because God forbade it. Yet another strike against Elyon.

I was more than happy to chat once I got over the weirdness of speaking aloud or thinking at Zilla in my head and having her reply. I wasn't sure how I felt knowing Zilla could sneak in there and listen to my thoughts, but on a positive note, I didn't get a creepy vibe from the living ship, more one of joy that Zilla finally had people to talk to. How lonely she must have been unable to communicate with anyone.

Even better, she offered me a more comfortable place to stay aboard her. A welcome offer seeing as how my apartment had been condemned due to mold concerns from the leak. The landlord made me wear a hazmat suit to collect personal belongings. Overkill if you ask me.

Once Zilla realized my situation, she immediately offered a solution: *"I have a room you can use."*

"Won't Tron be pissed you invited me aboard?"

"Only if you're in his way." A snarky reply.

I couldn't say no. And so I learned to beam without puking. Even better, I didn't lack for anything. Zilla outfitted me with clothes, fed me, and dropped me wherever I needed to go, which turned out to be around the world in a literal blink of an eye. But the thing I appreciated the most? The information Zilla shared.

I found myself fascinated by Elyon and his heavenly home. Images showed him as grand and regal as well as varying in countenance. According to Zilla, he could take on any appearance he chose. The only thing that remained the same? His glowing eyes.

When asked, she listed all his accomplishments and included his habit of meddling with planet ecosystems to create suul, which he had his angels collect, a practice that curdled my stomach. From what I could tell, we were his livestock, and upon our death, he profited.

But Elyon and his farming of Earth lost my focus when Hell was spotted at the outskirts of our solar system. Zilla saw it well before the Earth telescopes did. Its appearance gave me the opening needed to start convincing religious sects outside the Templars that we needed to join forces.

It didn't entirely surprise that most mocked me when I told them Hell was coming. I expected it from some religions, their beliefs too firmly entrenched to listen to a woman who had no actual proof. But even the Catholic church refused to listen! Efforts made to convince them failed. They didn't see Tron as an angel come to help us but a demon. Jesus Christ could have helped, but he kept turning down our requests claiming he had other business to attend to.

Metatron refused to make further appearances stating, *"I am not an object to be bandied about and have his existence disputed. If they don't want to believe, then they will suffer the consequence."*

He had a point. We didn't have time to waste.

Given their refusal to join the Templars in preparing for battle, they were kept out of the loop as we—and by we, I meant mostly me—made plans. Despite having lost my job, I had no free time at all between my ambassador duties and supervising security for the hidden military installation that acted as a base of operations. Turned out my dad hadn't been crazy after all when he sunk our savings into buying the large plot of land.

As an added bonus, the abandoned facility—which he'd picked up in an auction when the military downsized—had two spaceships that were being worked on for evacuation. While no one really discussed it aloud, we all knew those two ships wouldn't be able to take more than a hundred between them. Our base alone had more than that. The sad truth? There didn't exist a ship big enough on Earth to rescue more than a few, not to mention we'd never even made it past the moon, let alone another planet. I never told the crew working on those ships about the futility. Hope was all we had.

I worked closely with Metatron, and we maintained the bickering, as if we couldn't resist as soon as we got close. His handsome butt would show up somewhere, and I'd have a go at him, and he'd be sarcastic right back. We'd part, only to be brought together again and again. I guess it shouldn't be any wonder he featured in my dreams—usually wearing no clothes.

Did I find him sexy? Heck yes. If he kissed me, would I shove him away? Heck no. But you wouldn't find me making the moves first. It just seemed like a bad idea. We were allies, nothing more. We couldn't afford the emotional distraction. Or so I told myself. A part of me wasn't sure I could handle it if I did make an attempt to seduce and he rebuffed. Best we kept things professional.

When the Templars sparred with the angels to improve our skills, I made sure to never be paired with him. Yet I'd have sworn he watched me. Unfortunately, the sessions usually led to me getting handed my ass. My petite size put me at a disadvantage in hand-to-hand combat.

Those grueling sessions annoyed because they wouldn't let us use guns. Tron called them unsporting. I scoffed at that logic. "According to who?"

"Killing should never be done from afar," he insisted.

"I thought you told us we could use slingshots and bows?"

"Because they require not only skill by the user but that the subject be in visual distance."

That caused me to snort. "Who makes these arbitrary rules?"

"It is known as fighting with honor."

"I'd rather live. Let me ask, what will Hell's forces be using?"

His lips pressed flat.

I prodded. "Well? Are they using swords and maces or something we've never seen?"

"You might have seen it," he muttered. He glanced to his left, and for a second, I thought he might lie "Recent reports have placed them using projectile weapons. Only instead of bullets, they fire energy that can evaporate flesh."

"You're kidding, right?" I gaped at him. "And we're supposed to fight back not using guns?"

"There is a possibility the combustion aspect of your weapons fails around some of Hell's minions.

They have many tricks. It's why you will learn to fight with your hands."

"Whoa. I want to go back to the part where you say our guns might fail. How is that possible?"

He roiled his shoulders, causing his wings to lift and drop. "Some of them are born with abilities."

"Such as?"

"Mind control. Levitation of objects. Force grip." He named off some stuff usually only seen in X-Men movies.

"Well shit," I muttered. "How is it that the demons here never used anything like that?"

"The ones you've encountered thus far have mostly been simple-minded imps. On Hell, they would have been culled for being a waste of resources."

I winced. "That's not nice."

Rather than reply, he said, "I think it's time you showed me how the Templars handle nests."

"If you insist. However, I don't know how long it will be before we find one."

"And if I could offer a location?"

"Sly, Tron, very sly. Okay. How big is it? Do we know how many demons?"

"Imps," he corrected. "That is the correct term for what the twisted and undesirable. Astaroth appears to have been encouraging them to multiply that he might take command of and use them to sow chaos." Astaroth being the demon prince stuck on Earth who'd been causing trouble. I'd heard stories of him second-hand from Lilith and Tamara, who'd both had run-ins with him.

"How can I tell the difference between an imp and a demon?"

"When you meet one, you'll know it," he promised. "Just be careful you don't listen to its lies."

A bit melodramatic so I rolled my eyes. "Imp. Demon. Whatever. I'll eliminate them both. So back to this nest you found that needs cleansing. What do you know about it? Got any footage?" Not necessarily needed, given Templars often went in blind, embarking on missions sometimes based on rumor alone.

"The cantorii placed the surveillance onto one of these little sticks that you might view it." He held up a USB device. I snatched it and loaded it into a laptop. There was a single file on it, a video, which I played.

It showed a rocky mountain, almost sheer. Three-quarters up it, a lip jutted and provided a door sill of sorts to a dark crevice. A cave, the most popular choice for a nest. Surprised it wasn't twigs in a tree? Don't be. Nest referred to the fact the imps liked to huddle in a mass. Some hung from the ceiling, but those that couldn't fly, their wings too stunted or weak, congregated on the ground, a stinking group of monsters who only came out to feed.

Most times the Templar sects managed to find them before they went through the local wildlife and started going after humans. The knights kept a close watch on news reports of animal attacks taking down large prey or going after entire herds without being seen. Soon as we had a suspected nest, we went in and wiped it out. Callous? Not after you'd seen your first monster chewing on a toddler who still clutched its teddy.

The video kept playing, the shadows moving rapidly, showing a time-lapse as the sun set and the moon rose. Its bare light allowed me to see a gray mishappen face peering out of the cave. The imagery zoomed past the opening to show a moderately sized space with about a dozen snoozing bodies.

Three snipers outside the cave entrance would be more than enough to handle it. Time to show Tron why his training in hand-to-hand was a waste. We should be practicing our gun aim on moving targets.

I shut the laptop and caught Tron's gaze where he stood across from me. "Okay, I've got what I need. We'll beam in four. Me, Joey, Kyra, and Monroe. We'll have Zilla drop us about a mile downwind of their location."

"Who is Zilla?"

"Your ship. Duh." How could he not know her name?

He appeared puzzled. "Our vessel is a cantorii."

"Whose name is Zilla."

He frowned. "Only arks have names."

"According to you. All I know is Zilla told me her name, and unlike you, I don't have a problem being nice and using it."

"I find it hard to believe you're communicating. After all, why would the cantorii choose contact with you over me or one of the choir?"

"Because your God put up some kind of a block that prevents her from talking to angels. Maybe you should look into removing it."

His lips went flat. "Perhaps I will. About your plan, there will be five beaming, as I'll be joining you for observation."

"Do you have to?" I was well aware by this point how the angels were a magnet for imps when they turned their HALOs on, which meant if he came with us we'd lose our surprise advantage.

"If I'm going to gauge how to best use the Templars in battle, I should see how you fight. And I can also intercede should you misjudge the situation."

"Still not sure why you're so intent on having us fight. I thought the plan was to blow Hell up before it got here." Over the last few weeks, it had been decided we'd try and nuke the shit out of the Hellroid heading our way. Now if only we could get some of the governments on our side. So far, only the Americans were talking with us, and by talking, I meant we had the ear of one retired Air Force general who believed in ETs.

"If the attempt to damage or divert Hell fails, you should be ready. Not to mention, Hell's scouts will be here soon enough, and they will be ruthless."

"Nastier than imps?" I queried with a lilt.

"Very. The scout ships will be carrying pawn demons, not their smartest but chosen because they are fast, wily, and ruthless."

The somberness of his statement brought a shiver to my flesh. "Then I guess we'd better make sure we're ready. What time should I tell the team we're going?"

"Now."

My brow arched. "What?"

Tron smirked at me as he said, "You won't always have the luxury of preparation. Grab what you need. We go now."

CHAPTER 6

Nothing like being given no notice for a mission. However, I wasn't about to argue with the smug-looking Tron. He expected me to complain. I wouldn't give him the satisfaction.

Instead, I got my ass ready. I jogged to my quarters while clutching the walkie-talkies we used in the underground base, barking instructions for Joey, Kyra, and Monroe to meet me by the exit fully geared. I ignored their questions by shutting off my walkie. I made it to my room only slightly huffing and entered to see the mess created by my stash of worldly possessions. All my weapons, some clothes, and the ragged doll my mom gave me that had gone with me everywhere. I gave Reggie a kiss on her almost bald head. Might be time to get the wool for her hair rethatched.

Despite Tron's urgency, we couldn't beam

directly from the base, not without possibly pinpointing our location. We'd had issues elsewhere with ambushes by Astaroth and his minions. I'd mentioned only once to Metatron that it felt like we had a traitor in our midst—and by midst, I meant his angels since only they knew where and when we were beaming. Tron shut down that line of accusation, saying, *"The choir would never betray."* I had my doubts about that. Everyone had a price.

My team and I exited the base and then hiked a half mile to the hidden hangar with cars. We drove the non-descript sedan for more than an hour before we met up with Tron waiting for us outside a power transfer station. I wondered if he'd chosen it because it jumbled signals.

The moment we disembarked with our gear a bright light encased us and we were transported. A good thing we'd had a chance to discuss our plan on the drive over. I'd briefed those coming with me on the nest and the fact this was our chance to show Metatron we could handle ourselves. We'd come prepared, our duffels loaded with rifles bearing scopes, binocular goggles, even a few grenades and smoke bombs. This wasn't our first imp rodeo.

Zilla dropped us in the spot I requested. Big tall trees, thick enough to climb and use as a sniper's roost. Easy enough for us humans to maneuver, not so for the big man with bulky wings. He scowled at the base of my tree, and Zilla spoke in my head.

"The principality doesn't seem pleased."

"He's just peeved he can't see from his spot," I muttered as I adjusted my perch, clearing small branches so I could properly straddle a limb, popping down a tripod to steady my rifle before I sighted through my scope. Zilla had put us in a great location. The sightline to the cave's entrance perfect.

"The principality is leaving the area," Zilla announced. A glance down to the ground showed the feathery end of him as he walked in the direction of the cave.

I couldn't exactly shout, not this close. Small noise might be unnoticed, but a yodel in the middle of nowhere? Let him get closer if he wanted. I'd cover his butt.

Twilight took forever to arrive, and as the sky went from purple to night, I positioned myself, eye to the scope, knowing the imps would come crawling out once the sun left the sky. While they weren't allergic to daylight per se, they preferred the cover of darkness.

My jaw dropped when I suddenly saw an angel rising in front of the rocky cliff until he hovered in front of the cave. What was that idiot doing?

Metatron landed on the slim ledge and strode inside the dark aperture, which led to much consternation from my team. My earpiece had Simon huffing, "Do we go in after him?"

"Hold your position." I wasn't about to jeopardize the mission because Tron couldn't sit back and let us handle this.

An imp emerged, scuttling out, its wings fluttering. As it leapt—*ping*—a shot took it in the chest, and it dropped. We fired on all the emerging gnarly bodies, our expressions grim, keeping silent but for the crack of the guns as we fired.

By the time the wave of monsters ceased, I'd counted more than the dozen I'd seen on film. Tron had yet to exit.

My lips pursed as my earpiece buzzed with Joey's voice. "Want me to go in and see if it's clear?"

"We'll all go, except for Monroe. You keep watch in case something goes in after us." I slung my rifle onto my back before I tossed down my bag and climbed down the tree. On foot, we headed for the base of the mountain, moving swiftly, conscious that Tron had yet to reply. I contacted Zilla by thinking hard.

"Zilla, can you get a bead on Tron?"

"Sorry, Francesca, my attempts to penetrate are failing past the entrance."

A reminder that for all her awesome abilities, Zilla did have some limitations. Even she couldn't see through rock. She required a line of sight. Maybe the cave went deeper than expected.

The mountainside had enough incline and grips for us to billy-goat our way up. The silence from the cave we approached proved daunting because I could sense it wasn't natural. As if something muffled sound. We reached the ledge and could only stand on it one at a time as we entered the cave, our headlamps turning on with the press of a button. Would it highlight us? Yes, but at the same time, we couldn't fight in the dark, and the bright UV aspect of it tended to annoy imps.

The nest I'd seen on video had no monsters left, just a scrap pile of fabric and bones from their meals. A glance overhead showed no imps hanging from the ceiling. Also no sign of Tron.

"Where'd the angel go?" Kyra whispered. She might as well have shouted the way the acoustics of the cave grabbed the syllables and bounced them, the muffling effect from outdoors not present inside.

"I don't know." I treaded deeper into the cavern, my light shining upon what at first seemed like the back of the cave, only as I neared the rocky surface, I noticed overlapping stone columns forming a passageway that went farther into the mountain.

I raised my hand and brought my crew to flank my back as I went in first, rifle at the ready. The jagged tunnel proved large, large enough for a big angel, but not without cost. A few feathers lay on the ground.

Tron had definitely come this way. Given the hairs on the back of my neck stood at attention, I kept my rifle slung over my back and gripped my revolver. At my hips I had knives ready to go should I lose my gun. I'd come armed to fight.

The muzzle of my weapon remained aimed in front as I navigated the tunnel, knowing the bobbing light on my head announced my arrival but not willing to sacrifice my visibility, especially for monsters that hated bright lights. Besides, chances were anything in the cave already knew of our presence.

Still, we did remain quiet as we followed the twists and turns to emerge into a vast cavern. At least three stories, maybe more, I gauged from my spot at the top of an incline with a narrow path that sloped down to the sandy shore of a lake. A lake well past the purview of the light emitted by my headlamp, and yet I had no problem seeing it in its entirety.

A strange bioluminescence, hueing pale blue, emanated from the walls and even the hanging stalactites, only the water appeared dull. A glance up and down didn't show Metatron or any imps for that matter.

A peek at my feet had me saying, "I don't see any droppings." No need to add that seemed unusual.

"I don't like this," Joey murmured as he stared at the lake, a crease between his brows. He'd eschewed the headlamp and instead carried a flashlight, which he holstered on his utility belt.

"Ominous place," Kyra agreed, her rifle up and

out, aimed. Given she never missed, I appreciated it, especially since I'd like her to be watching my back as I went down to the shoreline.

"Metatron came this way." I pointed to a single feather caught on the stony arch before the ledge and ramp. "I'm going to look for him. Kyra, you wanna stay and cover while Joey and I check out the bottom?"

"That's a long walk back up," Joey lamented.

"Bah, I used to do more stairs when I was living off campus during college," I boasted. He did have a point though. My thighs would be screaming.

"Not sure why we're doing this. Pretty sure the big angel can handle himself," Joey's complaint as he led the way, his sure steps heading down the steep incline that showed no recent signs of use. No shit or skid marks from the imps or anything else for that matter. It seemed kind of odd nothing used the cavern as a lair. Perhaps the strange illumination most likely kept creatures away, or was there something we'd yet to see, something dangerous?

Had Tron encountered it? I saw no sign of a fight as we neared the bottom. No scattering of feathers on the gray and beige mixed sand. No splotches of blood or bodies of any kind. Just a smooth beach.

I didn't like it. Foreboding chilled me to the marrow. Poor Joey wanted to leave. I could see it in how he kept looking behind us when he wasn't intent on the lake. He truly thought the threat would come from the water. It seemed most likely. The question being, would I be better off handling it with my rifle or my revolver?

Guess it depended on how fast an aquatic monster could hump itself onto the sand to attack.

The smooth beach stretched around the circumference of the lake without a single ripple or water line left from any waves. The surface of it remained utterly still, and yet it didn't reflect the ceiling.

"Don't touch the water," I advised.

"You couldn't pay me to get close to it," Joey swore. "That's got nasty written all over it." He'd chosen to pull his sword. He was one of the few who'd already known how to wield one before the whole thing with the angels happened.

Joey and I kept a space between us, while remaining close. Hopefully, Kyra, our sniper, would handle anything before it reached us. Our heads constantly swiveled as we scuffed across the sand.

I was primed for attack, yet I still jumped when a very low voice said, "What a lucky day for me. Who should I eat first?"

Whirling, I beheld a man, of sorts. Sinfully beautiful, with the chiseled features seen on the covers of magazines, his hair a dark tousled mop. His upper body muscled and sexy. His bottom half that of a hairy beast with hind quarters ending in hooves. His forehead pierced by two curling horns. It could be only one thing.

"Demon!" I exclaimed.

"You don't say," a dry reply. The demon cocked his head. "How curious you can move. Your friends had no problem obeying me."

A glance showed Joey frozen in place, his eyes unblinking but looking utterly terrified. Given Kyra didn't shoot, I could only assume she'd been affected as well. "You can't fool me with your tricks, demon."

"How modern of you to judge me by my appearance. You know, I used to be able to live in the world until my heritage became too pronounced to hide." He stamped a hoof. "My prince and father, Astaroth, commanded I hide until the coming. But it's been years since my exile. Years of only rare companionship. My children aren't very good at bringing me live specimens."

"Your children?"

"Don't act so surprised. You met my chaos-filled progeny before you took their lives. A good thing I'm fertile and they grow so fast."

"Your monster-making days are over, demon," I swore.

"Really? And who is going to kill me? You?" His lips curled, and his pupils suddenly went vertical.

When he blinked sideways, I took a step back and aimed my revolver, which, for some reason, made him smile much too widely for my liking.

"Go ahead. Shoot." He held out his arms. "I dare you."

Despite dreading the reason why he gave me permission, I pulled the trigger. Nothing happened.

Click. Click. My dry firing ended up drowned by booming laughter. "Humans never learn. Which is why I don't understand how you can all be so dumb and yet, somehow, you always manage to win. But not for much longer." The demon paused to glance overhead. "Hell is coming at last."

"And you think they'll want someone defective like you?" Yeah, I probably shouldn't have said that aloud.

His expression turned stormy. "I am not broken."

"Says the demon whose daddy banished him to a cave. I'll wager you barely rank above an imp."

The hiss I got in reply braced me for the rush as he threw himself at me.

My hands gripped the hilts of my daggers, but I was too slow. They hadn't cleared their sheaths when the demon slammed into me. We hit the ground hard, with me as the cushion on the bottom.

Oof.

Air cascaded out of me, and when I inhaled, I gagged on the fetid breath of the monster with his beautiful face inches from mine.

"You smell delicious, but I think instead of eating you, I'll use your womb to replace those you killed." It writhed against me, and I readied to beg it to tear out my throat instead when, suddenly, liquid hit me in the face, hot and sticky, also thick.

Blood.

Ugh.

I spat and gagged and shoved at the body lying heavily atop me. Something heaved it off, and a hand grabbed hold of mine to haul me to my feet.

I coughed and hacked and wiped my grimy arm across my face until I could see Tron's smug face as he said, "And that's why you don't bring a gun to a demon fight."

I slapped him.

CHAPTER 7

"You hit me!" Metatron huffed indignantly. He'd not expected the resounding and rather strong slap. It didn't hurt, but it did offend.

A filthy Francesca glared at him. "You totally deserved it and worse. You did all this on purpose and almost had me killed. You lied. You knew the demon was lairing here and didn't warn us!" she groused as she shoved at the hair sticking to her face.

"Not a lie, merely an omission because you needed a lesson on cockiness."

"I did?" She sounded incredulous. "You're the one who needs a lesson on being a team player. We're supposed to be on the same side."

"We are. However, you kept questioning why I wanted you to learn combat skills other than firearms. I thought it best if I showed you why. It should also be noted that not all demons are the same. Their range of skills will differ. This one appeared to have an ability to control minds. Probably how he survived in here. He most likely had the imps bringing him whatever he needed."

"He said Astaroth was his father and that he was abandoned here because of his appearance."

Metatron nodded. "That would make sense. The Hell prince would be the only one capable of siring a demon."

"And demons make imps."

"They do, but imps can also procreate amongst themselves. And rapidly. It's why it's encouraged to remove nests as soon as they're noticed."

Joey suddenly exhaled as the thrall holding him captive released. "Fuck me, that was not cool." The man sprinted to the ramp, determined to escape despite the threat being eliminated. Francesca didn't show the same urgency to leave and kept haranguing.

"That was a dangerous stunt," she stated, lips turned down in displeasure.

"But it proved effective." He now had three witnesses as to what they could expect from Hell. Sometimes rumor could move more quickly and accomplish more than a boring lecture. One of his educators had been a proponent of hands-on training because he claimed experience trumped knowledge.

Francesca toed the body. "Why isn't it disintegrating?"

"It will, but demons take longer than imps."

"Why?"

"Because." He'd never cared to explore that question. He just appreciated the fact that, once dead, they cleaned themselves up.

"You are a shitty teacher," she complained, stalking for the slope back to the exit.

Rather than wait as she did the long climb, he darted for her and swept her up one-armed before launching himself.

She squeaked and grabbed hold, not just arms around his neck but legs around his hips too, bringing her intimately close. It startled enough he veered slightly on his ascent. His wings extended and flapped hard to correct, allowing them to land at the top of the ramp. Kyra had descended partway and kept an eye on Joey as he climbed.

To his surprise, Francesca didn't immediately let go. She held on and tilted her head. "You're lucky I didn't want to do that climb, or I'd slap you again for grabbing me like that."

"Go ahead and hit me." He dared her.

Her lips pinched. "You are so annoying."

"The feeling is mutual." He set her away from him before he entered the tunnel, ready to get back to the open sky. He'd gotten past the first bend in the passageway when she dared to duck around him to plant herself in front of him.

"What is your problem with me?" she huffed.

"I have no problem."

"Are you sure? Because you don't treat anyone else the same as me."

"And how do I treat you?" Other than at arm's length, for a good reason. He still felt the imprint of her against his body.

"Well, for one, you argue with me all the time."

"I do." He didn't even deny it.

"Why?"

"Because no one else does." The truth. It proved a novelty to have someone like Francesca who didn't look at him and see someone to automatically obey. She stuck to her opinions, right or wrong.

She pointed from where they'd come. "That was a dick move letting us walk into a trap. I could have died."

"I was there to ensure nothing untoward happened."

"What if you'd missed, or the demon was faster?"

"He wasn't."

Her gaze narrowed on him as if he'd given the wrong answer. "I won't have you pulling dangerous stunts like that. Nor will I be allied with someone who would take a chance with our lives."

"Sometimes the best lessons are the ones that make a deep impression."

She poked a finger in his chest, and he took a step back, mostly because his initial urge was to grab it and bring it to his lips.

"Listen here, if this partnership is going to work, I have to trust you."

He loomed over her to snap, "It goes both ways. I tried to tell you about the guns. You didn't believe me."

Her lips pressed flat before she offered a grudging, "I was wrong. From now on, if you claim something, I'll take it more seriously."

"You should because angels can't lie."

She looked him dead in the face as she said, "You just did." With that, she stalked off, the light on her head bobbing to light her passage.

He joined her in the first cave, where she used a stick to poke through the remains of garbage left behind.

"There's human bones in here." She pointed with a stick.

"Imps are meat eaters."

"Speaking of meat, I could use some food," Joey exclaimed, emerging from the passageway with Kyra. "That was some scary shit."

Kyra nodded. "One second I was scanning the beach, and the next, I'm like a frozen statue and there's that goat dude standing there. How did he do that?"

Despite it seeming obvious, Metatron stated, "He made himself invisible."

"Wait what? Demons can do that?" Francesca blurted out.

"Like I said in the cavern, demons have different abilities. Camouflage is a common one. However, for most it's weak and can't handle movement of any kind."

"What other powers can they have?" Kyra asked.

"The enthralling, which you experienced. Some can cast fire or ice. Others can wield air and use it to lift, squeeze, push."

"Just like Vader," Joey breathed in excitement.

Metatron had no idea who this Vader was. "Many demons also disrupt certain technologies when in proximity, like combustion and even chemical reactions."

"Meaning guns could be useless." Kyra lamented.

"In close range. A missile shot from afar will remain in motion even if the area around the demon nulls the ignition of accelerants."

"Hence why you recommended crossbows," Francesca murmured. "I think I need to do some more studying." She glanced at Joey and Kyra. "You guys ready to head out?"

At their nods, and without asking his permission, they exited to the ledge and were immediately beamed out. A moment later, so was Metatron, finding himself aboard the ship in his quarters.

His first question? "Where's Francesca?"

The ship showed him her location, along with the others, at the transfer station getting in the vehicle they'd left behind.

"Why am I not with them?"

The cantorii didn't reply. Couldn't. Or wouldn't. He'd bet on the latter, which meant the order to leave him behind must have come from Francesca.

He'd made her angry, and now she punished him. He'd only meant to show her a real demon so she'd understand what they faced. But did she appreciate the lesson he'd taught? Of course not. Humans could be so emotional about things.

Let her sulk then. Rather than rejoin her at the base, Metatron remained aboard the cantorii trying to better understand humans. Which proved impossible. He especially didn't grasp how Francesca thought.

He waited for her to contact him. Surely, she'd want his input on matters. By now she'd have grasped he'd done her a favor.

She ignored him, forcing Metatron to go to her. He used the pretext of important news, hiding his pleasure at the sight of her—gleaming with sweat as she trained with others on the crossbow.

He'd drawn her aside and announced, "Zakai and Tamara found Noah's ark."

Her response? "I hear we lost Jesus Christ because he was a traitor. That's going to make convincing people to fight with the angels a lot harder."

"You already know?"

"Zilla told me. Apparently, she's already made friends with Atlantis." The name of Noah's ark.

"Unfortunately, the demon prince escaped."

"I'm aware. He's a tricky bastard. Which is why I need to get back to training, so if that was all you had to say…"

Actually, he had plenty more he wanted to discuss. Such as why, when apart, she filled his mind. Yet, when together, they couldn't help but fight. He didn't hate her. On the contrary, Francesca intrigued him on so many levels it frightened. He didn't have time for an entanglement. Never mind others in the choir had partnered with humans. Metatron couldn't afford not only the distraction but he had to be very careful because anyone close to him could be targeted by Elyon. Just look at the trouble Jesus caused. Metatron didn't want to think anyone in the choir would betray. However, at the same time, he couldn't be sure if their duty to God would outweigh that to their angel brothers.

He left Francesca to her training and did his best to ignore her for a few days. Days where he couldn't stop thinking about her to the detriment of everything else.

When he finally couldn't handle the silence and strove to find an excuse to seek her out, he got one in the form of the base being attacked. He arrived in the aftermath, the imps having fled, leaving a swath of destruction—and bodies. It chilled him to see the still forms, but none of them Francesca, not yet. No angels died in the attack, but the transport vessels were destroyed. The base compromised. The time had come to relocate.

The stink of smoke permeated, ruining visibility. It took longer than Metatron liked before he found Francesca, unharmed and barking orders as an alarm blared.

"You need to evacuate," he declared as he neared her, his relief more intense than expected.

She barely spared him a glance, but her tone held a sneer as she replied, "You don't say, Captain Obvious. In case you haven't noticed, I'm already working on getting people to safety."

"You too," he insisted.

"When my people are taken care of." She waved him off.

Dismissed him.

It stung.

Metatron stalked about, as if he could be relevant. However, his skills were in waging wars, in sly maneuvers and deadly retaliation, not the evacuating of injured or the packaging for transport of supplies.

Given he accomplished nothing, he returned to the cantorii and paced his chamber. Distracted when he should have been focused.

All because of a woman.

"OPEN UP TO ME."

The sudden hammering demand from God sent him to his knees. Elyon projected himself at Metatron's HALO, the effect amplified since his ordinance differed slightly from the others in that it had a much wider range. A super HALO if you would. Ignoring God would only make things worse. He let God into his head.

"My scion hasn't reported in quite some time. What's happened to the Jesus assigned to your mission?"

"He's dead." Metatron knew he couldn't hide it.

"What?" Elyon exclaimed. *"Damn those humans."*

Metatron didn't correct the misassumption. Elyon didn't know of Noah and the ark they found. He'd prefer to keep it that way, especially given Elyon's other orders.

"This is your fault." God chided. *"I told you that planet was trouble. And yet you've neglected to handle it."*

"I'm working on it."

"That's not what I commanded!" Elyon hissed. *"You were told to abandon it."*

"But if you—"

"There is no argument you can make to sway me. You will turn my holy fire on its moon at once."

"Don't you think destroying the planet is kind of drastic? What of the people? At least let us wait for an ark."

"Why would I bother? I've already told you they're no good to me in their current form. That's the problem when you leave a garden untended. The weeds take over. Hence why there will be no ark. My previous order stands. Eden is to be destroyed before Hell arrives and steals its bounty."

"This is a mistake. There's much to treasure," he argued, attempting anything to belay the order.

"All of it tainted. I want nothing of it. You are to leave everything on that planet, do you hear? I don't want a thing from it lest the taint spread. Do you understand?"

"I do. I have to go. I'm needed." Metatron couldn't keep pretending to obey. He had a suspicion that Elyon already knew of his disobedience. But did he realize the choir had mutinied with Metatron?

It made him think of a conversation he had with Noah when he finally deigned to make contact.

Apparently, Noah, too, had chosen to go against God's orders and didn't regret his decision, even though it cost the lives of his choir. Noah claimed to mourn their loss but also said, "I cannot blame the humans for rebelling against their overlords. After all, why do we get to tell them how to live? How to act?"

Metatron's reply, "Look at what they became."

"I have. A world that is free. Free to decide if they're good or evil, perhaps sitting in between. They've accomplished wondrous things."

"Horrid ones as well."

"There are many sayings on earth that can be summarized as simply, how do you know what beauty is if you've never seen ugly?"

A question that stuck with Metatron. How did he know Heaven was the most perfect place? All the angels said so. But few had anything to compare it with. So how did they know for sure?

Metatron had traveled more than many and while he'd never seen a place quite like Earth, he'd been to some nice planets. Even a few space stations. Heaven and Hell, even the planets with flocks, weren't the only livable places in the universe. Honesty would even force him to admit that had someone told him he'd be forced to settle on Heaven permanently, he might have refused. The supposed perfection grated on him when he spent too much time.

In that respect, Earth, with its constant surprises, did make him feel alive. He could also see its potential. Not to mention, the thought of killing everyone, of destroying billions of people and all they'd accomplished, didn't sit right.

Metatron wasn't the only one to feel that way.

Rather than obey God's cruel command, the choir chose to act as their conscience dictated. Rather than participate in humanity's demise, they would help them and, in doing so, help themselves. A free Earth would make a sanctuary for angels who couldn't return to Heaven.

A home. But only if they could save it, and for that, Metatron needed the people of Earth to be on his side, meaning it was time for him to be more involved. To put himself on display and convince the powerful leaders of this world to join him in fighting.

The decision led to him asking the cantorii, "Where is Francesca? I need to speak with her."

Rather than answer, the ship moved him, and he found himself in a room aboard the vessel, with a very naked woman about to pull on a robe.

She whirled and blinked. "What are you doing here?"

"The cantorii brought me," he stammered as she hid her curves with a loose flowing garment. Too late. The beauty of her remained seared in his mind.

"Not cool, Zilla," she muttered under her breath, tying the sash. "Did you need something?" she huffed, flipping back her hair.

"How did the evacuation of the base go?"

She shrugged. "As well as expected. Zilla helped me spread out the people amongst other sects."

"Do we know how Astaroth's minions found it?"

"Does it matter? He hit at the heart of our rebellion, knowing it would demoralize people."

His lips pursed. "Making our task harder." Because convincing people to fight required hope.

"I'll figure something out to rally them." Her shoulders slumped. "Was that all you wanted?"

"Actually"—he cleared his throat—"I need to speak to your president."

Her head lifted sharply. "Since when? I thought you refused to do public appearances."

"Recent events with Astaroth have made it so I have to be more proactive if we're to stay ahead of his attempts to sabotage."

"About time you realized that. But here's the problem. I can't arrange a meeting with the president. We'll have to aim lower. Say like a cabinet minister or someone high up in the military."

"You mean the people who haven't yet managed to convince anyone to listen?" his sarcastic retort. "We tried your way. It failed. Time to go to the president directly."

"The president doesn't take appointments with just anyone."

"We are more than just anyone."

She sighed. "You want to just show up, don't you?"

He grinned. "It would make, as you call it, an impression."

"It would. Can it be tomorrow, though? I'm kind of tired."

She looked it, the circles under her eyes deep and purple. Exhaustion had her pale as well. If Jesus hadn't been a traitor who'd gotten killed for his actions by Noah's ark, Metatron would have used him to give her a boost.

But he didn't have the scion, only himself—and a power he'd been hiding for a long time because Elyon would have killed him if he knew Metatron had figured out how to use suul.

"I can help," he offered.

"Is this one of those kinky sex things where you think your dick can cure me?"

"I simply need to place a hand on your flesh. Any part of your body is fine. A connection is all that is needed."

"I swear if you yell praise God and slap me in the forehead, I will kick you in the balls. I know you have some," she threatened.

"This won't hurt," he promised. He held out his hand and waited. She slid her slender fingers against his palm and the contact sizzled with awareness for him.

He wasn't the only one who sucked in a breath. Their gazes met, locked, and remained that way as he opened himself to the ability he'd discovered by accident when he'd almost died on a mission. He'd been fighting some bugs on a flock planet when the ambush hit. In the melee that followed, he'd gotten knocked senseless and woke in a burrow, wrapped tight in a cocoon.

In his panic, the power just seared out of him, ashing the strands and sending him falling to the ground. He was the only one to escape alive. Elyon called it a miracle. But Metatron knew otherwise.

Over time he'd experimented to realize he wielded something similar to the scions—a power to heal, but he could also destroy. Since his arrival on Earth, he'd never felt stronger. All that suul begging to be used.

He held Francesca and willed his holy spirit, the only word he had for it, to do his bidding and ease her discomfort.

The tension in her released first then a breath, and when she exclaimed, "Oh, I haven't felt this good in ages," he let go, but their gazes remained locked, and Francesca smiled at him for once. A radiant curve of her lips.

Blame the intimacy of healing, the fact he'd been denying himself since they met, but he couldn't resist. He dragged her close, lifting her on tiptoe to brush his mouth against hers.

CHAPTER 8

I'd been kissed—and much more—by Tron before. In my dreams. But the real thing?

Wow.

Blame the fact my awareness of him kicked up a zillion notches when he took my hand in his. His subsequent healing had me feeling energetic—and aroused. When he put his mouth to mine, I ignited.

For weeks I'd been fighting my attraction to him, but now that he embraced me, his mouth slanting over mine, teasing and coaxing, I couldn't shove him away. I grabbed hold of his shirt and made sure he couldn't stop.

The kiss turned into one of panted breaths and nips. Tongues sinuously played. My body rubbed against his, his erection evident despite our clothes.

I reached for him, and he groaned, "We should stop."

I stepped back despite my desire to keep going and said, "If you insist. I don't need you to finish." I stared at him, a dare in my gaze.

He growled. "Why can I not resist you?"

I couldn't help teasing, "Because I'm perfect."

"You are everything," he growled.

He didn't have to reach for me. I threw myself into his arms, and this time, our kiss didn't end, even as we fumbled at each other's clothes.

My robe hit the floor in a puddle. His clothes took a little more effort, and they ripped in their removal. I had to admit to being excited at how eager he appeared.

He walked us back to the bed, the backs of his knees hitting it and indicating he could sit. He did so but ensured his hands on me maneuvered me into his lap. I sat sideways, my legs over his, his hard erection pressing against my ass.

To say I was wet would be an understatement. As his fingers threaded my hair to cup my scalp and keep our lips locked, I squirmed in his lap, already hungry for the end game. But he seemed content to kiss me, angling my head to give him deeper access, his tongue plundering and sliding against mine.

My hands couldn't stay still. They cupped his cheeks as I tasted him. They roved his body, tracing the contour of his shoulders, skimming over firm flesh, nails dragging and teasing. He growled, "If you don't stop touching me, this won't last long."

"Good because I hate to wait." I'd never understood guys who bragged about taking hours to give a girl an orgasm. Did they suck at it? Me, if I wanted to come, I wanted to come. Now. Not in an hour when my skin was rubbed raw.

I turned in his lap and properly sat astride, this time trapping his cock between our bellies. His hands palmed my ass cheeks and stroked the flesh but only for a moment before he used them to lean me back, projecting my breast.

He took a nipple into his mouth, just engulfed it and sucked. I quivered so hard I almost came. I did squirm and moan while he kept me arched, teasing my breasts, sucking them, nibbling the tips, grazing them with his teeth, driving me insane with pleasure.

I wasn't the only one moaning, though. He hummed as he played with me. Groaned when I reached between us to grab him.

My what a handful. It would be tight. And he'd go deep. Just the way I liked it.

His hand found its way between my thighs, and he stroked my nether lips.

"I want to taste you," he murmured.

I shuddered. "Oh, I'd like that, but I'm way too far-gone to last more than a lick." I leaned my forehead to his. "I want you inside me."

His turn to tremble.

I lifted my body and grasped his cock firmly, my

thumb stroking over the tip, spreading the pearl of liquid pooling. I rubbed the slick head of him against me and moaned.

I'd never wanted anything so much.

I guided him to my pussy and let go, sliding my body slowly down onto his cock. My sex pulsed in welcome around him. He was thick. He stretched me and filled me, and I couldn't help but squeeze as he hit just the right spot. It was all I could do not to come. But I held off.

I'd not dreamed of this moment to come in three seconds flat.

His fingers once more dug into my ass, and his lips found the flesh between my shoulder and neck for a suck. I rolled my hips, and he groaned. I ground against him, driving him deep, and it was my turn to pulse and catch my breath.

It felt so good.

I rocked and pushed against him, rubbing the very tip of him against my sweet spot. My breath halting, my heart racing, my body trembling with need.

My orgasm wouldn't hold off for him. I came.

Hard.

And shook with it. His hands were there to keep the wave of my climax going, pushing and pulling me to keep up the thrusting, rolling me into a second orgasm where he joined me.

I felt the hot spurt of heat as he came. Heard his

shout of enjoyment. Felt the crush of his arms as he held me tight. Sensed a connection to him that whispered, *You're what I've been waiting for.*

A moment of perfection that I didn't want to end.

When he finally stirred, I expected him to be aloof, abrupt, even dismissive of what happened. I'd learned angels didn't put as much stock in intimacy and sex as humans.

To my surprise he said, "Thank you."

"You're welcome?" Like what else should I say? I remained cradled in his lap and arms, limp with pleasure and not wanting to move. Not yet. Let me bask a moment longer before the brush-off.

His hand stroked down my back, and I shivered. Dare I say, my sexual desire stirred already. I'd never had that happen before.

"I'll have the cantorii move your belongings to my quarters," he suddenly stated.

I stilled. "Why?"

"I'd say that's obvious." His hand cupped and squeezed an ass cheek.

I liked it, a lot, and I was kind of peeved my feminist side just had to tartly retort, "It was just sex. Nothing more. No need to move in together." That was what I said. Inside? Melting marshmallow that he'd made the first move.

In any new relationship, getting past that first awkward "I like you" proved to be my downfall. The few times I'd put myself out there, I got shot down. A lot of men didn't like a woman like me, brash, able to fight her own battles, not willing to accept bullshit. Add to that the non-Templars saw me as too assertive and secretive, with reason, and one couldn't exactly tell a guy, *I fight monsters in my spare time.*

"So date someone who knows," you'd think. Only once had I disastrously dared to date another knight. It ended because he couldn't handle my imp kill rate was higher than his. Oh, and I never chose him as a mission leader. In my defense, it wasn't because we were fucking at the time but because he sucked when in charge.

"It was more than just sex, and you know it." He leaned back enough to look me in the eyes. "If what ignited between us were just about bodily release, we would have handled it upon first meeting."

"Maybe you would have," I snorted. "I'm not a slut to sleep with strangers. I prefer to get to know someone first."

"And now that you know me?" A soft purring query.

"You're not all that bad." Why did I not tell him the truth? How I thought him commanding, and yet caring. His plans did their best to minimize civilian casualties. He never asked anyone to do something he wouldn't do himself. He was also crazy sexy.

"And I'll be even better now that we'll stop fighting every time we see each other."

The statement caused me to frown. "Are you saying you argued because you've been wanting to screw me?"

He brushed a hair from my cheek. "We argued because we fought against fate. We are meant to be together."

I arched a brow. "Don't tell me you believe in soulmates?"

"I didn't until now."

He sounded so serious. Me? I wasn't sure what to think. This seductive Metatron didn't resemble the cold one I'd come to expect. I kind of liked it, though, the way he became someone more intimate for me. However, how did I know this wasn't a con? Maybe angels were players and I shouldn't read anything into it. "Good sex doesn't make us partners for life."

A hint of a smile played around his lips. "Maybe not, but it certainly is a part of it."

"I didn't get the impression you were the kind of guy to share his space."

"Usually, I'm not. I like my privacy. But I find myself, of late, not enjoying it as much. My thoughts have been consumed by someone." His gaze on me let me know who he meant.

I shivered.

"You're cold?" His arms tightened around me, and the warmth almost had me sighing against him.

Why did he have to say all the right things? Why couldn't I believe the lie? I couldn't wrap my mind around Metatron's change in attitude. His confession and claim discomfited. Us, meant to be? We couldn't be more opposite.

A shove had him releasing me, which surprised. I'd half expected I'd have to demand he let me go. I disengaged our bodies, immediately missing the warmth, my body pimpling at the loss. A rolling wetness seeping down my legs provided a reminder we'd not used a condom.

I grimaced. "I guess it's a good thing I'm on birth control since you didn't pull out."

"Angels do not use contraception," he admitted.

"Ever?" I blinked at him. "Aren't you worried you'll make babies?"

"Giving life is a blessing."

"Says the guy spreading his seed but not sticking around to be a daddy to the product."

"Warriors don't raise fledglings. We are obligated to turn them over to the creche the moment they return to Heaven."

"A creche being?"

"Where the fledglings are raised until they are of age to be assigned a caste."

It sounded cold and led to me asking, "If the

babies are being raised in a nursery, what about the mother?"

"Once the child is taken, there is usually no contact afterwards. Non-angels are not allowed on Heaven."

"But half-breeds are?" A crude way of saying it.

"There is no such thing as half. If the child was created by an angel, then it is an angel."

"The more you talk, the more I'm glad I've got an IUD," I muttered.

"You do not wish to have progeny?"

My nose wrinkled. "I've never been with anyone long enough to really think about it. At the same time, I'm not sure if I'd make a good mother. I'm kind of old at just over forty."

"Age doesn't have to be a factor," he retorted.

"Really?" I almost followed that topic of interest. But the baby thing still hung over us. "Truth is, I don't want a kid. Not right now. I might change my mind later if we survive this mess, but for the moment, it's a big-ass no. Knowing that, are you still sure you want to call me your soulmate?" I asked as I found my robe and slid it over my body.

"What I want to do is strip and explore every inch of your body."

My hands stilled on the sash I'd just finished tying. Every inch of me flushed, and I almost screamed *YES*. Instead, I focused on his reason for coming to see me in the first place. "Were you serious about finding the president and getting her to listen?"

"Diplomacy through proper channels is taking too long. It's time we took more drastic measures."

"Ambushing the president could get you shot and killed."

"Only if I'm caught." Spoken with a grin.

Be still my heart. Tron had a dimple. I almost climbed onto his lap to kiss it.

I turned away so I could think. "We'll need to track her movements and find a time to beam when she's less likely to be heavily guarded." I glanced at the ceiling, even though Zilla technically inhabited the entire room. "Can you start watching the president of the United States?"

"Already begun."

"Thanks, Zilla."

Tron eyed me oddly. "You were talking to the cantorii."

"Yup." I cocked my head a moment as Zilla imparted some info, which I related. "She says you can, too, if you get rid of the HALO."

His lips pinched. "I would like nothing more, but I can't. Not yet."

"Afraid your God will get mad?"

"Oh, he's already very angry, but removing the HALO means cutting off contact. I need to maintain it as long as I can for information."

"What kind of info? You worried Heaven's going to come smite your butt for disobeying?"

"Maybe. Elyon has a vengeful side."

"So much for being the God of forgiveness," I uttered as I whirled and caught an eyeful of naked male perfection.

Tron had risen from the bed to stretch. "He takes those who oppose his laws very seriously."

"And do you oppose them?" I asked.

"Very. But until now, I've not been able to do anything about it."

"Why not?"

"Because everything answers to Elyon. Angels. Arks. Cantorii. How can you ferment a rebellion when everyone is either too afraid or unable to show allegiance?"

The honesty in his answer struck me. "You want to rebel?"

"I already have, and Elyon caught me. It's why I was sent on what should have been an endless voyage, only we found Eden. A planet with so much possibility."

"I don't understand, if you wanted to get away from your God, why didn't you disconnect the moment you left? Why tell him about Earth?"

"It's hard to hide when you have a spy aboard relaying everything." He rolled his shoulders. "Jesus reported to Elyon."

"And he's dead now. So why keep chatting?"

"Because Elyon already knows about your planet. He wants it destroyed."

"Why would he do that? I thought we were a treasure chest of souls."

"He fears you."

I couldn't help a snort. "Not sure I believe that."

"There was a time I'd have scoffed too. I've seen purges before. Cleansings for new beginnings happen as colonies degrade and start to act out against their shepherds. But what he wanted to do to your world? Eradicating it entirely and not even taking the suul? It's unprecedented."

I stared at him in thought, my mind putting pieces together. "He's worried even the souls are tainted."

"Perhaps he does; however, I disagree. In my view, humanity has evolved into something unique. It's why I want to save them. Save this entire planet if possible."

"And if you can't?"

"I have to if I'm to protect the one thing I desire above all."

"What's that?" The question whispered from me.

"You."

CHAPTER 9

THE PROBLEM WITH HONESTY?

Sometimes it blurted out too much.

In a moment of weakness, Metatron admitted how he felt about Francesca. Why bother hiding it? It had only led to fighting and estrangement as they sought to ignore their mutual attraction. The bliss he'd experienced when they finally gave in to their desire made him regret the time they'd wasted.

She clapped and shook her head. "Wow, that's quite the line. Bravo. I'm impressed. The Bible never mentioned angels were slick playboys."

He frowned. "I don't understand."

"You don't need to feed me all kinds of cheesy lines to sleep with me. You want us to have sex, then fine. We'll fuck. I could use the release since I forgot my vibrator when I moved out of my apartment."

"That's rather crude."

"It's honest, Tron. You're right. There is an attraction between us. And given the end of the world might be nigh, why not play around and have some fun? But at the same time, we have to remain focused on the main mission. Saving planet Earth."

Why did one have to cancel the other? "That is still the plan."

"Good. Then we should get back to work on it."

With a nonchalance that irritated, she turned from him and played with the holo system on board the cantorii. Completely blasé, which was when it hit him. She pretended their coupling meant nothing.

Let her. For now. Later he'd show her why they were meant for each other.

"What are you looking at?" he asked, nearing her manipulation. He eyed the many images of a tall building from numerous angles and frowned. "Those appear to be of a singular location."

"Zilla's saying this penthouse is the best option to ambush the president."

"That seems premature to decide given the surveillance just began."

"Zilla started watching the president a while ago. Apparently, she predicted we'd want this sooner or later and so has been keeping track of the president's schedule and location."

It showed forethought of a level even more advanced than an ark. Or at least those he'd worked with. Having had some contact now with the very aged Atlantis, and its distinct personality and ability to make decisions, he realized Elyon had controlled the narrative—and his subjects—even more than he suspected. Did he even now assert some power over Metatron? Maybe he should go ahead and remove his HALO. But how much of a disadvantage would they have if he forfeited their only way to learn what Elyon planned? God wasn't the kind to hide. If he chose to come after Metatron, he'd say so, if only to ensure he had time to dread.

"What is this location, and why is the cantorii suggesting it?"

Still not looking at him, Francesca replied. "Zilla says the president visits almost weekly, sometimes twice, not for too long. And she gets there via convoluted methods. There's actually a tunnel from another building, a remnant of an abandoned subway line, that leads to this condo." She pointed. "The elevator for the penthouse takes her straight up."

"Who is she visiting?"

"No idea. The owner of the condo is a corporation, but if I had to guess, Madam President has a lover."

"And she feels a need to hide it?"

"The people might have elected a widowed woman to office, but they are strange when it comes to them being sexual beings with needs. Hence the subterfuge, which is great for us because, during those visits, she is out of the public eye, and her security isn't allowed inside the condo. They're left in the basement where she enters the elevator."

"Leaving her unguarded."

"Not entirely." She manipulated the floating images and pointed to windows first. "They're missile-proof, one-way glass."

"My divinii blade can cut through it." Very little could stop its slice.

"You'll set off an alarm if you do." She continued to show him the defense. "Roof has motion cameras and sensors. The elevator requires a key card and only stops on three floors. Lobby, the basement, and the condo itself."

"None of which matter if the cantorii beams us inside."

"So, fun fact, she's already checked and can't find a way in. The place is airtight." Which meant no beaming as the cantorii needed some kind of access to project particles.

"There is always a crevice."

"If there is, Zilla hasn't found it yet."

Metatron remained undaunted. "These alarms you speak of, they run on electricity?"

"Yes, but if you're thinking of cutting power to them, they have backup batteries."

"But they are electronic?" Rather than wait for a

reply, he added, "If we emitted a magnetic pulse, it would ruin their ability to function."

"You can create an EMP?" she asked in excitement. "How much of range? Could it do the entire building, maybe even penetrate to the basement? If we could block the Secret Service from getting to her by knocking out their coms and the elevator, that should give us the time needed for a face-to-face with the president."

"The cantorii can pulse the entire city if you want."

"Just the building and the street around should be good. We'll have to prepare to go at a moment's notice since the president doesn't schedule those visits."

"I'm ready," he stated.

She eyed him, and her cheeks turned pink. "Hardly. You're naked."

"You should be too."

His hand went to her sash, and her mouth rounded. "We should be working on our plan."

"We did. We have one. Now it requires waiting but no reason to be bored." He tugged the knot and parted her garment.

Her breath caught. "But we just did it."

"That was just an appetizer." He, for one, felt hungrier than before.

Her lids half shuttered, and she licked her lips.

"And what do you have planned for the second course?"

Apparently, nothing because the cantorii suddenly flashed an image of the president getting into a car.

To his disappointment, Francesca shoved out of his arms and showed interest in what the cantorii announced.

"She's going to meet her lover," she announced. "We've got about twenty minutes. Better get ready."

He was ready all right. He spun her toward him and kissed her.

Her surprise lasted only a sharply indrawn breath before she kissed him back, murmuring, "Make it quick so we can cleanse before we dress."

He groaned, mostly because he couldn't have gone slow once her hands started stroking him. She grabbed hold of his shaft and rubbed it, their height difference not letting her put it where they both wanted.

He palmed her waist and hoisted her, her legs tucking around his flanks and under his wings. Her sex taking his cock with a heated squeeze that had him bracing lest his knees collapse.

Their lips remained locked as he bounced her, his hands on her buttocks, buried to the hilt, their breathing matching in raggedness as they both raced to orgasm.

The moment she climaxed, her channel milking

him hard, he joined her, jetting deep, feeling her contractions, the rightness of the connection.

Their joining ended with her soft kiss on his chin and murmured, "We have to get going."

While he hated having to cut the intimacy short, he did enjoy watching her as she extended her arms and spread her legs for the cleansing.

They dressed, both of them adding layers of garments and weapons. Her more than him. He didn't recognize the knives she strapped on. Had the cantorii provided them? He knew the ship couldn't replicate the firearm she holstered, meaning Francesca had stashed some on board. Wouldn't Elyon have a fit if he knew?

When they were both ready, he hooked his arm around her waist and the cantorii beamed them to a spot above the building, hidden inside the damp clouds. Francesca clung tight, as if fearful he'd drop her.

Never.

She murmured against his ear. "Zilla says the pulse has knocked everything out on that block."

"Then let's go meet your president." He angled through the moist cumulus layer and emerged closer than expected to the towering complex. The windows he sought were a mirrored bank that showed him arrowing in. Nothing he could do about that. His one arm tightened around Francesca as his other pulled his divinii blade.

Before hitting the glass, he pulled up slightly and hovered, his wings beating steadily while his rapid slices created an opening, the glass he'd carved falling inward. He flew through and deposited Francesca as he surveyed the room.

A woman and a man eyed him with dropped jaws.

The president, recognizable from the images he'd seen, recovered first and blustered, "Who are you? What is the meaning of this? Is this a joke?"

Metatron touched the pommel of his sword to his chest in a sign of respect as he said, "I am archangel Metatron, warrior in Elyon's Army of Light, here to give you warning that your planet is about to be overrun by agents of Hell."

CHAPTER 10

I couldn't blame the president for laughing at Tron's announcement. It sounded insane. It didn't help the media had been buzzing of late with angel sightings and imp issues. People were convinced of a massive-scale prank. I had only to recall my skepticism to know the expression on the president's face indicated she wouldn't be a person easily convinced.

She crossed her arms and gave Tron a steely-eyed gaze. "Accosting me is a crime."

"Hardly accosting," Tron replied. "Merely relaying important information. Your world is about to be invaded."

"Sure it is and you're a real angel." The president rolled her eyes. "Nice costume."

I cleared my throat. "Crazy as it sounds, it's true. And trust me, I was a skeptic."

The steely gaze swept to me. "And you are?"

"Francesca Moretti. Leader of the Pittsburgh Templar Knights, sworn to fight evil. I've been trying to organize the defense against Hell."

"Hell?" The president snorted. "I think my agencies would have noticed an invasion of demons boiling from a crack in the Earth."

"You mistake where the threat is coming from. Hell is in space," Metatron corrected.

I jumped it. "It's that meteor they spotted entering our galaxy. The really big one."

The president waved her hand. "It's never going to hit us. My scientists say it's going to end up in the sun."

"They're wrong." A flat reply by Metatron. "Hell will change course shortly. Before it arrives, though, you'll have to deal with the legion it will send to pave the way."

The president uttered a short bark of laughter. "This is priceless. You want me to believe Hell is coming as an alien invasion."

It sounded insane, and yet I jumped to his defense. "He's telling the truth."

The president crossed her arms. "Prove it."

Before I could say a word Metatron's HALO ignited. He pointed, and a bright light enveloped them. My eyes closed against it, and when they opened, he and the president had disappeared.

The man she'd been meeting gaped. "He evaporated her."

I hastened to reassure. "She's alive. Just elsewhere at the moment. Tron's giving her the proof she asked for."

The man shook his head and muttered, "Angels and aliens. I need a drink." He turned for the bar, a man with silvered hair, broad shoulders, and a confidence that would have appealed if I didn't only have lusty eyes for Tron. "Want one?" he offered.

"I'm fine." For now. I reserved the right to get royally drunk later if we survived this meeting. How had it not occurred to me that the president would be so skeptical? And what was Tron thinking, kidnapping her? I could only hope it didn't backfire—

He reappeared with a visibly shaken president, who didn't ask but snatched the glass from her lover's hand, downed it, and held it out for more, which he poured.

"Well, that was eye-opening," the president murmured. It hadn't seemed long to me, and yet she returned with a haunted expression.

Metatron inclined his head. "Apologies for the abruptness of my actions. However, it seemed more expedient than wasting time talking."

"Most people make an appointment instead of accosting me outside normal channels." The president sipped her second glass of alcohol and appeared more composed than a moment ago.

I shrugged. "It's one of those things where

you've got to believe it. Trust me, I had a hard time in the beginning too."

She tilted her glass at Tron. "There were other ways. Pretty sure him landing on the front lawn of the White House would have gotten my attention."

"He'd have been shot before he touched foot," I retorted.

"He's really an angel?" Her lover was the one to question.

Tron pivoted without being asked and flared his wings.

The president added, "I saw his spaceship and another of his kind. Angel or alien doesn't matter. He's definitely not from here."

"Will you hear what we have to say?" I asked.

The president nodded. "Tell me everything."

By the time we'd summarized the main points, the president was rubbing her forehead. "I couldn't have a normal term, could I? Dammit."

"So you'll help?" I asked.

"Of course, I don't see any other choice if what you're saying is true. But I think we should be open with the people about it. Once they realize that asteroid is coming here, panic will hit. We need to come out strong and confident. Let them know we're handling it. Once law enforcement can't keep up with the crime, it will be utter anarchy."

"We need something to rally humanity." Metatron stated the obvious.

"This kind of threat might, if handled right," the president murmured, her gaze lost in thought.

"People coming together to fight an asteroid?" I couldn't help but sound skeptical.

"The common person can't actually participate, just follow along on whatever strategy we use to break it up or shift its path."

"There is one thing they can do," the president's male companion interjected softly. "They could pray. Religion could unite the world."

The president shook her head. "I don't know if it will happen. Maybe a few decades ago when things were less polarized. If we fight, it might be on two fronts, one trying to keep the population from imploding and the asteroid." She fixed on to Metatron for a sharp, "How many angels did you bring?"

"A choir," was his useless reply, as no one knew exactly what that number was.

"By choir, he means not many," I admitted.

"We'll need as many as can be spared if we're going to convince other countries to coordinate with us."

Tron frowned. "The choir has duties already."

"And they shall keep doing those. I'm talking about being visible to the public. It wouldn't hurt if they did a few heroic things and got seen doing it," the president explained. "We can talk further about this at our meeting. I'll have my staff set aside a time for us to gather. Bring a few more of your angel friends. We might need them to convince my generals."

Judging by Metatron's face, he did not appreciate the brush-off. I grabbed his arm. "Thank you, Madam President." Despite the rough start, this meeting had gone better than expected.

"Don't thank me yet. We still have a military complex to convince."

We left the same way we came, and only moments before a secret service helicopter landed on the roof to extract the president. Zilla beamed us back unharmed, but we didn't celebrate—naked—yet. Metatron called a meeting with his choir, which included a few human faces.

He told them of our upcoming meeting with the president. Asked for status reports on everything else. We heard the Atlantis had begun loading passengers and already was starting to have issues with people trying to sneak past the perimeter set around the massive ark, which covered a massive space and yet cast no shadow. Its exterior could blend in so seamlessly it felt as if the sun's rays hit your face. The only reason you knew it was there? It occasionally turned off the camouflage and hovered. Long enough for people to take pictures of Atlantis. Long enough for those in its shadow to tremble. If it fell... Smush.

Was it wrong I kind of wanted to see it? I didn't

ask Zilla, mostly because I didn't want her to be jealous if went to see the ark.

We discussed what it would mean to work with the American military to form an offense. We'd have access to much heavier artillery, if the generals didn't shut out the angels. We also had to contend with the possibility the missiles would fail. If the nukes didn't blow up Hell, we had to be ready to fight when Hell reached Earth.

The observation was made once again, this time by Eoch, a grim angel. "We need more than just the Americans fighting. What's happening with other countries?"

"Each one is different," Metatron grumbled. "Efforts to have them listen have been met with ridicule."

I snapped my fingers. "You need legitimacy. Someone to declare you're real and not fake."

"This disbelief in humans..." Tron shook his head.

Lilith, who'd shown up for the meeting with Aziel, had a perspective from her specialty in communications. "In this age of social media, you need something to make you go viral. Something like the most followed religious figure in the world."

I gaped before blurting out, "If we convince the pope that gets us a foothold in all kinds of places."

"Once we've got that locked in, we can work on other religions," Lilith offered as a solution.

"How do we arrange a meeting?" Tron asked.

"Have you reached out at all to the Vatican since your arrival?" Lilith queried rather than replying.

"Overtures were made and rebuffed. I believe some of those exact words were Begone Satan." Metatron looked utterly nonplussed as he added, "I chose to not waste my time."

"Well, we'll need to do something about it now. Having the pope and then the president declaring the angels real will trend, and other countries will be looking to their leaders." Lilith's hypothesis.

To it, I added, "Even if other governments don't join us, they'll be looking to protect the planet. Their people will demand it."

"We mustn't forget that some will think they can bargain with Hell." A soft reminder by Metatron that Jesus Christ betrayed them.

The meeting ended, and everyone filed out. When I would have, Tron held me back, and I thought it was to further talk about the upcoming invasion until my back hit a wall and his mouth was on mine.

Needless to say, I came quick again. I swear the angel only had to touch me and I was halfway to orgasm.

Those orgasms were the only good thing to come out of those next few days. We spent the days waiting for our meeting preparing and dealing with increasing issues as we went viral but not in a good way.

Images of Atlantis had begun trending, along with the word apocalypse. It led to a mass exodus to that desert location. Drones and even a spy plane from across the ocean, which was shot down, made it dangerous, and so the ark removed itself. Operation Eden Two stalled as they sought a new location to bring people in secret.

To counter the apocalypse trend, the angels began making appearances, the most noteworthy being when Munna saved a child from a burning building. The image of him striding through the smoke, his wings partially extended, his HALO lit, carrying the little girl went viral. It didn't help the apocalypse trend but rather amplified it. It didn't help that the imps had been causing trouble of late. People saw little difference between the angels and them, which bugged Metatron.

"How can they not see we are good compared to their evil?" he'd railed.

Because people only saw what they wanted. Narrow lenses didn't allow for a wider view of things.

Still, I could only hope as a second day passed that the president hadn't changed her mind about meeting with us. Would the most recent videos of imps causing havoc convince her? They'd been attacking boldly of late.

On the third day, the summons arrived. Six of us went to the White House. Our meeting with the president—call me Jane—went as expected with only a slight surprise. She indicated that Astaroth, the Hell prince, had approached her and tried to parlay. Luckily, she didn't choose to pursue that deal and appeared to have her generals eager to fight. The war machine at work. But in this case, we needed it.

The president told a country of millions—and by extension a planet of billions—the coming threat. Even showed some trimmed footage offered to give her some credibility. While she worked on uniting a country to prepare for war, others focused on Atlantis and its evacuation effort—with millions already screaming it wasn't fair it could only take a select number. I didn't envy Tamara and Zakai, the pair in charge of Atlantis, their job. Wrangling people sucked balls. But Metatron handled it like a pro.

Watching him make plans was the sexiest thing. He let me join in on every meeting he had with the American army. At the same time, as we coordinated with them, we sent out feelers to Europe. They were coming around but had demands if they were to join a coalition.

Demands?

As expected, Italy refused to have anything to do with anyone involved since the pope had declared the angels and their message to be fake. The proclamation went viral and caused some of our United Kingdom talks to suddenly collapse.

"That false prophet is causing problems," Tron declared, pacing the room we shared. Yes, shared because once we started screwing there seemed no point in fighting it. I saw no point in denying myself the pleasure of his company. The angel knew how to make my body sing hallelujah.

I lounged on his bed, naked and sated—for the moment. "When isn't Astaroth causing issues?" I grumbled. It seemed the demon prince couldn't stop getting in our way. I was just glad his plan to steal Atlantis failed. If we didn't stop Hell on Earth, it would be up to the ark to ensure some remnants of humanity survived.

"Astaroth is annoying but not my current irritation. I'm talking about the charlatan claiming he's the voice of God."

"Wait, are you talking about the pope?"

"Yes. Blasphemer!" I'd rarely seen Tron so worked up.

"What are you going to do?"

He whirled on me. "I don't know. But he has to be stopped. He's splitting our ranks at a time when we cannot afford to be divided."

"Killing him will only make him a martyr."

"It would be quickest," he grumbled.

"But not solve our problem. We need the pope to recant and declare your mission holy."

"By taking him like I did the president."

"Actually, that's not a bad idea." I tapped my chin.

"I thought kidnapping was bad."

"In this case, though, talking won't work, and it would be expedient. It's not like you're going to hurt him. You're just going to give the pope an epiphany of faith. Beam in to see him. Take him to Zilla for a tour. Maybe fly him around."

"He is more corpulent than you. It might not end well."

"Dropping him would be bad," I agreed.

"Then I shall endeavor not to."

I cocked my head as Zilla suddenly spoke.

"The place the pope lives is blocked from my sight. I can't beam into it either."

A dead zone. It could happen apparently with some artifacts that used to be aboard the Atlantis but got scattered before the ark went to ground for a long nap. Not surprising the Vatican would have a holy relic.

"So he'll have to fly in," I muttered aloud.

"Are you taking to the ship again?" He arched a brow.

"Zilla says the area around the Vatican is a no-beam zone. We'll have to wait for the pope to leave before you pop in to grab him."

"Does he go out often?" he asked.

I waited for Zilla to answer and then repeated, "She says every other day."

"I don't know if I want to wait. The need to unite the world grows with each day as the commandments are ignored."

"You can't be seriously thinking of going in. Why not instead think of something to draw him out?"

"Because that will take time."

"At least wait until night. You're less likely to be shot out of the sky," I insisted.

"That's in two hours," he stated without even looking at a watch. "I should do some surveillance."

"In the daytime? You'll be seen. I should go and map us a route inside."

"We both know flying is the best option, and for that, I'll want my hands free."

"You can't go alone."

My lips pursed even as I thought to Zilla, *"I'll need a weapon so I can provide backup."* Only then did I reply. "I'm coming, and that's final."

"You have a devious look about you," he replied.

"It's called my game face, Tron. The one I put on when we go do something stupid but heroic to save the world."

CHAPTER 11

THEY BEAMED TO THE ROOF OF AN APARTMENT BUILDING high enough in the bright sunlit day that no one could see them arrive. At times Metatron wondered why transport had to be such a bright beacon that made it hard to be stealthy.

The roofing, smoothed by years of rain, gave little grip, and Francesca slid when he set her on her feet.

She steadied herself and looked around at the city spread out before them. "I'll bet those in the penthouse pay a pretty penny for that view."

"If they're alive." He pointed to some scat. One of many piles. "Imp fecal matter and it's recent."

Her nose wrinkled. "I don't want to know how you can tell. It's foul enough already. Guess they took a breather here on the roof. They must have a nest in the area."

"Given it's daytime, more likely they're inside." Metatron pointed to the door with the scratch in it.

"Wait, you think they're squatting in apartments? What about the residents?"

His lips flattened. "Most likely dead."

"We should go take care of them." She didn't even hesitate. Her courage rivaled his own. It didn't help with his fear: what if she got hurt?

He had to wonder though. "Why are the imps here in this city? It's much too populated for them to live here easily." Most preferred secluded areas where they were less likely to be hunted.

"Maybe they came to see the holy city and pee on its walls." She made an interesting point. Imps could be rather bestial in many respects.

"Or they're here at Astaroth's behest to make our task impossible. You said killing the pope would make him a martyr. But what if it were done publicly by imps?"

Her expression turned thoughtful. "By God not intervening in some divine way, it would allow Astaroth to claim he doesn't exist. Take away the hope of Heaven and salvation, add in Hell ponderously approaching, and the result will be utter anarchy, which, in turn, will hinder our efforts to repel the asteroid."

"Exactly."

"Assuming you're right. Could be they're just dumb imps who got lost and found the closest spot to nest. Doesn't matter. We'll handle them so they don't hurt anyone else. I assume they'll exit at sunset. I'll take up a sniper position in line with the door. As they emerge, I'll pop them. Those that get missed will be yours to handle."

"Or we could let them out and see where they go."

"You want to see if they're after the pope," she accused.

"I want to see if they have a motive for being here. As should you."

"You think Astaroth is behind their presence."

"It seems more likely than them randomly ending up in sight of the palace."

"Why do I get the impression you're not upset by their presence?"

"Because we can use them to our advantage. The pope refuses to believe we are sent here from God, but he might be more amenable if we were to save his life from actual demons."

"It would be taking a huge risk. What if they get to him before we can?"

"Then he dies and we convince the next to take his place." It seemed simple to Metatron. He even preferred that plan to saving the man causing so much trouble. The pope should have been the one person who just did as told by the choir.

"We don't have time for the games the church plays when it comes to succession, not to mention the next one might be just as disinclined to side with us."

He sighed. "This whole making people believe is much harder than it should be."

Francesca patted his cheek. "Welcome to a world where thoughts are diverse."

It led to him grimacing. "A bane and a boon all at once."

"You're starting to get us, I think," was her laughed reply.

They hunkered to wait. At least she'd not suggested they infiltrate the apartments. That would have put them walking into an unknown situation, putting her in danger.

As they waited, he couldn't help but fall into a memory of his most recent conversation with God.

Metatron had wanted to ignore the insistence buzzing from his HALO. A HALO that he alone still wore. The others in the choir, after hearing what the so-called blessing had been doing—spying on them, giving out their location, possibly even influencing—chose to have theirs removed.

Not Metatron, he'd kept his for one reason, to talk to God. It made sense at the time, but when that the reason signaled, he half wished he'd done like the others. Anything to not deal with the unpleasantness he would now face. However, ignoring the summons wouldn't make Elyon go away, so he had answered.

"Hello."

"Hello? That's all you have to say?" asked the deceptively smooth voice, the reception clearer than it should be. Not a good sign. Heaven wasn't supposed to be anywhere close to this galaxy. "You continue to disobey me."

It could only mean Elyon knew Metatron had chosen not to abandon and destroy the planet as ordered. Metatron had hoped with Jesus Christ's death—the scion being Elyon's nosy eyes and ears—that his actions would evade detection a while longer. However, Elyon always did have his sneaky spying ways, some of which Metatron had yet to discover. "Yes, I disobeyed because your orders were unreasonable."

"That wasn't your decision to make. The Eden flock is corrupt. It needs cleansing."

"It's not corrupt. It just doesn't want to be your vassal. And I can't say I blame them. You've done nothing for this planet."

"I gave them life!" God boomed, and Metatron held in a wince as the words reverberated in his skull.

The discomfort hadn't stopped him from growling, "And now you would punish them for living as they see fit."

"I banished you so you'd stop causing trouble."

"You banished me because you knew if you tried to order me killed, I'd make sure Heaven saw you for what you really are." And it wasn't the genial God they worshipped.

The next statement was practically spat. "Your mutiny and that of the choir won't go unpunished."

"Really? And how do you plan to mete it? It would require you leaving your precious palace on Heaven. Which we both know won't happen, not with Hell practically on Eden's doorstep."

"I've tolerated much from you, Metatron, but this time, you've gone too far."

"I could say the same. I should have put a stop to your megalomania a millennia ago." Before Elyon got so strong.

"You were weak then, and you are weak now."

"Am I? I dare you to say that to my face." A challenge tossed.

"As you wish," the ominous reply.

The connection had severed, and Metatron had sighed with the realization there was no turning back now.

Earth was going to war. And Hell might not be its worst threat. How could he tell Francesca, though? Or anyone else for that matter?

"Are you okay? You seem bothered." An intuitive Francesca noted his discomfort.

"Just pondering my next actions and thinking it's time I removed my HALO," he admitted. If only to stop Elyon's intrusion into his head.

"I thought you want to keep an eye on your boss."

"I do, and yet it goes two ways," he muttered.

"Then ditch it."

"Easy to say. It's been a part of me for a long while."

"If it helps, its removal doesn't seem to have bothered the others."

She referred to Zakai and Elija, the first two to get rid of theirs. Munna had recently followed, and Eoch had been talking about it too.

"It's hard to give up something that's been a part of your identity for a long time." He still remembered his pride at being chosen as part of Elyon's army. It took a long while for the novelty of it to wear off.

"Then keep it, but know so long as you do, he might be watching, listening, plotting, and tracking."

He sighed. "I know it has to go. I'm just struggling with it. The breaking of vows should never be done lightly."

She put her hand over his. "Then think about it a while longer if you must. I wouldn't want you to regret it."

He already did, so many things he'd done in the name of his God and Heaven's laws. The words of a rebel from long ago came back to haunt him, more than ever before, *Who decides what's good or evil?*

It used to be he trusted Elyon with that task. But doing good shouldn't have left him feeling uncomfortable and full of regret.

In companionable silence, they sat and waited. As twilight fell, they gave each other a long embrace before readying themselves. Francesca lay on her stomach with her weaponry set up on a tripod. He perched on a humming metal machine, square in shape, with vents to draw in air.

Before the oranges and purples had faded from the sky, the door slammed open and the first imp emerged.

Pop.

With methodical precision, Francesca shot the imps, rarely missing. A gun jam led to her cursing and clicking as she sought to fix the issue. He swept in, sword at the ready, scything through the imps that hissed and snarled in his direction. More of them than expected.

It meant a few managed to escape, flapping off in the direction of the Vatican.

Pop.

An imp fell, and a glance showed Francesca switching to another weapon. "Go after the ones escaping. I've got the stragglers," she announced as she began firing again.

He hesitated. Leave her alone to fight? Or trust she could handle herself?

The latter proved harder to accept but the right choice. Only two live imps remained on the roof, and he detected none coming through the door, so he took off, pushing hard with his legs to launch into the air. His rapid flaps quickly closed the gap between him and the fleeing imps but not fast enough to catch them as they aimed for a balcony allowing entrance into the Apostolic Palace where the pope lived.

The pair of imps flitted inside, and he was ready to follow them when a scream from behind had him swiveling his head to see a cloud of flapping wings heading for the palace. By now, the guards stationed had noticed the aerial invasion. They shouted as they took aim. However, the handful of snipers couldn't keep up with the descending horde.

He diverted his path to attempt and save the soldier grappling with an imp. As he got close, the imp stared right at him, hissed, and tossed the man over the wall before throwing itself into the air. It didn't get far before Metatron's sword sliced it in half.

Metatron alit on the parapet and held his ground as some imps arrowed for him, throwing themselves on his blade, as if they wanted to die.

It hit him in that moment that they purposely caused a distraction. The imps weren't here for Metatron.

He jumped back into the air, wings extending with a snap as he arrowed for the balcony where the imps kept entering. He heard shouting and then, more alarming, a cloud of the creatures emerged, and they weren't empty-handed. He counted at least two cardinals with their red hats and robes, but of more concern, they also had the disbeliever in white.

He couldn't let them kill the pope. To that end, he ignited his HALO and called on his shield. It encased him stronger than he'd ever managed before because of this suul-rich city. He drew on that power and funneled it to his sword, which gleamed with holy wrath.

His wrath.

He boomed in a voice learned on the battlefield. "Unhand the holy man, foul creatures."

The pope's eyes widened as they fixated on the glowing Metatron.

The imps hissed and then dropped the pope, who shrieked, only to be caught by a different set of imps. Who also dropped and caught. The creatures played a game and drew attention. People appeared to gawk from windows and on balconies. They converged in the street as well, staring upwards at the unfolding drama caught in the roving spotlights the guards manipulated.

Gunshots rang out, and an imp fell, along with a cardinal.

The male in question didn't scream when he hit the hard ground. Pulverized on impact.

It led to those watching exclaiming in horror. Metatron had to stop this.

Metatron hovered and projected his voice. "Unholy creatures, you have gone too far. Unhand

His Holiness at once." He used the honorific cognizant because he wanted the pope—however annoying—on his side.

The imps cooperated a little too well, letting go of the pope, who plummeted with a yell that cut off as Metatron only barely managed to grab hold, slowing his descent. He dropped the pope in a courtyard full of armed guards, who quickly circled the man.

He'd deal with him after he handled the imps facing him with slavering jaws and extended claws.

For some reason, a human expression slipped past his lips. "Bring it."

The imps took it as an invitation to fight, and not only did they all converge on him at once, but they also dropped the remaining cardinal. This one didn't splat but rather hit a roof and rolled, only barely catching a ledge. He'd better hold on because Metatron didn't have time to rescue.

As the imps swooped in on Metatron, he took care of them, slashing and slicing, his body in continuous motion, his shield holding steady despite the many blows. Given the way they crowded, he landed atop a turret to battle, jaw gritted as he hacked, the imps seemingly an endless wave despite their dead bodies turning to ash.

It took all of his strength to keep fighting until he went to swing his sword and realized no imps remained. He took a moment to lean on the pommel of his weapon and surveyed the area around him. The sky appeared clear, but given the darkness of night, that didn't mean anything. He heard no screams, but he did note the murmur of voices and see the many cameras aimed in his direction, taping his actions. Good. Let them see an angel fighting evil. It would make it harder for the pope to deny their existence.

Speaking of whom... He returned to the palace, landing in the courtyard and facing a pair of guns aimed at him.

"Where is the pope?" he asked.

One soldier swallowed hard before saying, "What are you?"

"God's voice on Earth. Now where is he?"

The soldier pointed at the palace and the door leading inside. Metatron didn't let the lock on it get in his way. He sliced his way through and found the disbeliever in white on his knees praying. "...Heavenly Father, forgive me my sin." The guards in the room appeared confused, some raising their weapons to take aim, others dropping to their knees and bowing their heads.

To avoid injury, he kept his shield and HALO raised as he announced, "God hears your prayer, but he has yet to forgive, given your impertinence in refuting his messenger and warriors."

His words drew the pope's startled gaze, which

quickly turned to fear, as he did the sign of the cross. "Get thee back, Satan."

"Hardly Satan," Metatron snorted. "I am an archangel of God. A warrior in his Army of Light."

"Prove it."

"It is not I who needs to prove his worth to God but you. Refuting his word. Ignoring his blessed warriors." He pointed his sword. "By challenging his choir, you have aided the enemy. Are you an agent of Hell?"

"Never," the pope blustered, struggling to his feet. "I am the holiest of men. God speaks to me!"

"That's a lie," Metatron's flat reply. "If you were listening to God, you would have never disavowed our existence. You would be aiding us in our holy battle against Hell instead of strengthening the enemy."

The pope refused to give in. "How do I know you're his angel?"

The repeated stubbornness had even the pope's own soldiers eyeing him with disbelief.

But looking at the sweating man, it hit Metatron. "You know I speak the truth; you just don't care."

"I do care," the pope huffed. "I care about living. Hell is coming, and Heaven isn't coming to help us. And a handful of angels won't stop it."

"We could if humanity joined us. If a religious leader blessed our mission."

"I'd rather take the deal Astaroth offered."

At that statement, Metatron decided he'd had enough of the traitor and blasphemer. He was also done catering to the non-believers who plagued his every move. He strode forward and grabbed the pope, dragging him outside.

No one stopped him. He leaped into the air, dragging along the squirming and shrieking pope. He rose high enough that the crowd gathering outside the palace could see him, hard to miss given how bright he glowed.

He held out the pope for all to see, his voice amplified as he announced, "People of Eden, I am Metatron, archangel and warrior in God's army of light, here to give you warning. The imps you saw tonight are only the beginning of the terror coming for you." He didn't need to look to feel the crowd's rivetted attention. After a slight pause, he continued. "Hell is coming. That asteroid in the sky is Hell's kingdom, and soon, you will face its army of darkness."

A few wails broke out along with moans. "What can we do?" someone yelled.

"Nothing," exclaimed the pope. "We can't stop—"

Rather than let the man finish, Metatron let go of the pope, who fell screaming toward a wide-eyed crowd. It would have been easy to let him die, but Metatron heeded Francesca's words and held out his hand, extending the power he'd long been cultivating in hiding. He slowed the pope's descent and deposited him on the ground, where the man proceeded to scream, "He's not an angel. And Hell isn't the evil we've been taught. We can bargain for our lives."

His words led to much murmuring and anger. Metatron heard more than saw those who spat and called him a Judas, which led to him saying, "God rejects this sinner." He pointed and focused his power to strip the robes from the pope, along with his cross, leaving him in his undergarments, looking weak. He then cast his gaze upon those watching and added in a whisper they all heard, "Who here will follow God?"

To his surprise, the cardinal who'd been dropped by the imps and managed to escape the precarious roof was the first to kneel. "I am the Lord's servant."

Metatron pointed. "Behold, the true believer and, as his reward, your new pope."

The man in red appeared surprised for a moment but soon nodded as he replied, "The church will aid in your fight."

"Will any others join the pope in battling the forces of darkness?" Metatron usually wasn't one for flowery speeches, but with this rapt audience, he could ask for no better time to convince.

"Tell God I am his loyal servant!" a woman screamed from a balcony as she fell to her knees.

Metatron pointed. "You are now a soldier in God's army."

"Me too!" a man by her side declared, also showing fealty.

Metatron extended his arms and said, "All those who bow now will be remembered after the coming war with Hell and will receive the reward of life." Not a lie. If they beat hell, they'd get to survive.

The singing began with a single voice, "Glory to God in the highest..." And then others chimed in, the overall melody beautiful. It almost covered the whining of the traitor.

"Do not listen to him. I am your leader. I tell you what God wants."

"False prophet." A man with scrubby whiskers spat.

"God sent his angel to remove the rot in his church," said another.

As the people below crowded the former holy man, others kept singing, their prayers and sudden belief almost visible in the air.

He'd done it. Improved Eden's odds in the coming battle. Wouldn't Francesca be so proud? Thinking of her led to him winging his way back to the rooftop where he'd left her, only to find it empty. No Francesca.

He glanced at the open door on the roof. Had she gone inside?

A few strides took him to the opening, reeking of

imp. Definitely no subtle perfume. Still, he went down a few steps, holding his breath, noting how the landing was too filthy to have avoided her leaving any steps. She'd not come this way.

He headed back to the fresh air and muttered, "Where are you?" Perhaps she was on board. He contacted the cantorii and asked to be beamed aboard. Still no Francesca.

It led to him grumbling, "Where is she?"

The cantorii didn't reply. Couldn't or wouldn't? Either way, the HALO had to go. Not being able to talk properly hindered.

It took a few deep breaths and a stilling of his psyche before he softly said, "Please remove my HALO."

The ship didn't answer, but it did act. The painful process didn't take overly long, and when it was done, he felt no different except for the voice in his head that said in a distinctly feminine tone, "*About time.*"

"Zilla?"

"*Who else would it be? And no time for niceties. You have to rescue Francesca.*"

"What happened?"

"*A demon took her.*"

CHAPTER 12

I had no problem with Tron taking off to go after the escaping imps. Actually basked in the fact he didn't pull some macho shit and recognized I had the situation on the rooftop under control, and by control, I meant I shot the monsters.

Bang.

Bang.

The gunshots cracked loudly, and with me standing to fire, the recoil packed a punch. Given I bruised like a peach, my shoulder would be a lovely color later if I didn't ice it. The imps I hit dropped and almost instantly turned to dust, such a handy feature when it came to cleanup. Nothing worse than trying to explain to an accidental witness that you hadn't just killed someone. A few even tried to go to the cops, but they ran into a dilemma when they couldn't actually produce a body.

The final imp charged me, hissing, a few greasy strands of hair jutting from its crown, its teeth missing in spots. Hideous fuckers and not one ounce of intelligence in those eyes. Now that I'd met a real demon, the difference proved startling. In questioning Metatron and Zilla about it, they'd explained that weak demons produced even weaker offspring. In simple terms, the less pure the blood, the more likely the product of a union would be born flawed, often with bestial traits that forced them into hiding. The worst of those were named imp. And once imps started reproducing with each other? They reverted to their most primitive state.

Which led to me wondering, what were such base-line imps doing here in the city in such great numbers? This wasn't a few random strays wandering in. I glanced around as if I could see in the darkness. Being in the city provided some illumination, but none of it far-reaching. The sky itself, with its clouds, could have been full of imps for all I knew.

A glance toward the pope's palace, and I could see the glow of Metatron's HALO, dipping and bobbing as he fought. How I wished I could join him, but I didn't have wings, and while close, I wasn't close enough to feel confident about taking shots. So much for being his backup.

"Zilla, can you drop me closer to the palace? Somewhere I can help Tron?" I questioned, only to get no reply. How odd. Usually, she responded right away. Maybe she was busy. At least I knew she could track me since she'd inserted a token inside me. A piece of herself so that she could always find me.

In the distance, I could hear screaming, the spine-tingling kind that spelled fear, and then abrupt silence. Metatron's HALO hovered, and in its glow, I could see the outline of imps, holding someone in white between them. Oh shit, the pope!

What could I do to help?

I glanced at my stash of weapons. My rifle lacked the range. I'd need to get closer, which would take time.

In that quiet moment of contemplation of my options, a whisper of fabric drew my attention, and I whirled in its direction. I froze at the sight of a strange-looking woman standing at the door from which the imps had spilled. She reminded me of Tim Burton's Corpse Bride, all giant eyes, long dark hair, pale skin, and torn white gown trimmed in lace. A gown spattered in red and brown stains. As she walked toward me, the rags undulated as if carried by a breeze, even as the air around me remained still.

A part of me screamed, *Shoot her.* Another part whispered, *Drop the gun. There is no danger.*

Thunk. Suddenly nerveless fingers loosened, and my weapon hit the rooftop. My gaze couldn't leave the stranger's. As she neared, I found myself frozen in place and only when I forcibly tried to look away did I realize she spoke inside my head. But worse than that, she controlled me.

"There's a good, tasty girl. Stand still for Isadora. Let me smell delicious terror. It's making my tummy rumbly. What a lovely meal you'll make."

Nothing like being told the tang of my fear made me palatable. The creature, for this was no woman, chose to walk around me, trailed by a carrion scent, not that I could gag. My limbs remained frozen. Only my horrified mind had free will, and it screamed this wouldn't end well, not with those fangs peeking from her upper lip.

"Daddy said not to kill you, but he didn't say you'd be so tasty." The woman licked her lips as she reached me and circled.

"Who. Is. Daddy." I managed to push the words past my lips.

Her lips widened into a smile that showed more than her prominent incisors were sharp. "As if you can't guess? Astaroth, the greatest prince to ever live. Soon, he will take his rightful place in Hell, and I will have my pick of delicious things."

As I fought the compulsion holding me, my tongue loosened, even as my limbs didn't. "Astaroth isn't a great prince. He's a loser who got stuck on this planet. Do you really think Hell's going to reward him for needing a rescue?"

"No insulting my daddy." The cuff to the head

rocked me, and I would have blinked back the tears at the sharp pain if I could move. Only my mouth had free rein.

"Your daddy is going to be in for a rude surprise, I think, as are you and your siblings. My understanding is Hell values perfection, and you"—I paused to draw it out—"are anything but. Or have you not looked in a mirror lately?"

A giggle spilled from Isadora, chilling and insane. "Daddy says I'm beautiful. He is going to make me a princess, and I will marry a prince. I shall ask for you as my wedding gift." The thing that I wouldn't call a woman stood before me, head slightly cocked, eyes completely mad, and stinking of rotted meat and shit.

"Assuming he is even going to bring you when he leaves."

"Daddy promised." Isadora stamped her foot.

"Everyone knows Hell princes lie."

I expected the slap but could do nothing to block it. My lip split, and I tasted salty copper. Lovely. This would probably make Isadora even crazier.

She sniffed and growled. "Oh, you are teasing Isadora. I must have a bite."

"Astaroth said to not kill me," I huffed quickly.

"Daddy said keep you alive, but he didn't say if you had to keep all your bits." She smiled wide, showing off the jagged dentition. "What should I eat? Face so you can't scream? A foot so you can watch?" She smacked her lips, and my stomach lurched.

I closed my eyes as she leaned close to murmur, "Call me ugly? Maybe I'll bite off your yummy nose." She pressed a moist kiss on the tip of it, and I almost pissed my pants.

Just as I feared I'd be maimed, a sharp male voice snapped, "Step away from the Templar, Isadora."

"But, Daddy..." The monster pouted, and my eyes shot open to see a man whose picture I'd memorized.

His name slipped from my lips. "Astaroth." The demon prince himself.

"Always nice to be famous," he said with a smarmy smirk. "And you are the Templar in charge who's been causing trouble. Do you know your particular sect has ruined the most imp nests of them all? On track to beat your father."

"What do you want?"

"Other than recognition and a triumphant return to Hell?" His smile widened. "I want to bring a present worthy of Hell's King. I hear Lord Satan is hard to please, but what better gift than the beloved mate of an angel?"

"I'm not his mate." Girlfriend maybe, but we'd never really spoken of our relationship and expectations for the future when we had sex.

"Does your lover know you lie? Maybe that's why he likes you. Or could it be he sticks around because you're a pivotal piece in this rebellion? I wonder what will happen when the Templars realize they've lost you."

Despite the chill in my veins, I kept my tone steady. "If I'm gone, others will step in to take my place."

"They'll try, but let's be honest, there aren't many like you in the Templar ranks. How many will turn coward without a strong leader to guide them? Want to wager that some will bargain with hell instead of fighting?"

I hated that his insidious suggestions wormed their way into my head. "There are more of us than there are of you."

"Which won't matter if they're all fighting amongst themselves. Humanity is so easy to mislead," Astaroth offered with a sly smile.

"And so are you. Look at you, eager to return to a place where you will be one of many princes. Giving up all Earth has to offer, and for what?"

"For ultimate power of course."

"You really think you can waltz back to Hell and be someone important?" I managed a derisive snort.

"I have a plan. And you're only part of it."

"I won't help you."

"Good. I hear Lord Satan likes his bedmates feisty."

Of all the things I expected to happen in my life, getting given to Satan to use as a whore never made the list. Then again, neither did falling for an angel or saving the world.

"I'll kill you before I let you take me." It wasn't just my mouth working now. My fingers could flex. If I could grab a knife, I could stab Astaroth in the heart, right here, right now.

"You'll try. Won't she, my precious?" My dumb butt had lost track of the Corpse Bride, and that proved my undoing, as fingers grasped my hair and wound cruelly.

I tried to contact Zilla, but my attempts felt muffled as if my calls were blocked. Most likely by the demon in front of me. I'd have to fight.

Shoving with all my might against the compulsion allowed me to suddenly gasp as her control severed. I moved quickly, pulling a knife from the sheath at my hip, and slashed, scoring a line across Isadora's thigh. Her shriek almost pierced my eardrums; worse, she didn't let go of my hair. A screech escaped me as she tugged hard, the pain sharp where she tried to scalp me. Isadora didn't just yank. She punched me in the lower back, hard enough I gasped and bent over. Before I could recover, she slammed into me, taking me to the rough surface of the roof, her arm pressing against my neck, her fetid breath washing over me as she panted in my face.

"Don't kill her," Astaroth warned.

"Let me eat her eyes. Pop them like juicy grapes," Isadora begged, and I almost puked.

"No maiming her. She's a gift to the Dark Lord. Hold her arms for me so I can secure her," the prince ordered his creepy daughter. Isadora grabbed me by the wrists and slammed my arms over my head.

Her order to keep still had me in its grip once more, and I couldn't even protest as the cuffs went on, the metal of them cold.

Isadora rolled from me and got to her feet before she yanked me to mine.

"Are we taking her to my lair?" Isadora asked.

"We aren't doing anything," Astaroth declared before slicing his hand through the air.

I blinked as one moment Isadora had a head, and the next, it went flying, right over the edge of the parapet. The body collapsed, as did her spell holding me.

In shock, I exclaimed, "You killed your daughter."

"She outlived her use," Astaroth drawled. "Time to go. I do believe Metatron is done playing with the decoys."

Decoys? AKA the imps. They'd flown off as part of a plan to separate us. This whole thing had been a trap. "How did you know we'd be here?"

"Because I have an inside source."

"Who?"

"Someone you'd never expect," Astaroth said

with a smirk. He glanced overhead and stated quite clearly, "We're ready to come aboard."

"Aboard what?"

A cloud of darkness enveloped us, not long enough for me to panic. I saved that when I could see again and found myself somewhere else.

"Where am I?" I asked, glancing around at the pulsing black walls and floor with their streaks of red.

"On the scout ship sent to retrieve me. Say hello to our pilot." A glance showed someone with four arms and eyes literally on the back of their head.

It waved.

I gaped.

The thing in front of the console chittered, the sound a series of clicks and whistles. Astaroth replied. "Yes, we can go now. I have what I need." His smile focused on me. "Since you're probably curious, we're on our way to Hell, a place no angel has ever dared to enter."

Meaning I could forget rescue.

Fuck.

CHAPTER 13

It took Metatron a second to process Zilla's announcement. "What do you mean Francesca's been taken by a demon?"

"Those imps and the attack on the pope appear to have been a ruse to distract and separate you."

The news rocked Metatron. "Why didn't you beam her out before she got caught?"

He could hear the sorrow as Zilla replied, *"I lost all ability to see or transport the moment the imps attacked."*

Meaning a demon, one strong enough to null signals in the area.

"I'm sorry," the cantorii said, and it was in that moment that it occurred to him they spoke. As in an actual conversation. To think, it never happened before because of the HALO. Now that he'd removed it, he felt no different than before other than the fact

he spoke to his vessel, an intelligent being as it turned out. It blew him away like a hurricane wind on the planet aero, a place of mostly gases and floating island balls.

"What a mess," he muttered, rubbing his face.

"She's still alive," Zilla replied. *"The token I gave her is emitting."*

"Wait, you know where she is? Beam me to her." He'd skewer the demon who dared kidnap his mate.

"I can't. She's been taken off-planet."

A chill swept him. "She's on a Hell scout ship?"

"Yes."

"Where is it? Show me." The air in front showed a zoomed-out view of the galaxy and a tiny dot moving rapidly from Earth toward the Hell behemoth. "Can we catch up before it reaches its base?"

"No."

He had no hope of rescuing her, something he refused to accept. "What are the options?" He asked Zilla because he didn't have a clue what to do. If this were just a random human, he would have felt bad and moved on. But this was Francesca, a woman he'd fallen in love with. Nothing, not the war with Hell, the mutiny with Heaven, mattered as much as her safety did.

"I can get you into Hell."

He straightened from his slump. "Won't they spot you and blast you to pieces before we get close?"

"My shielding and cloaking are excellent."

He almost said, "Let's go," only to remember risking the cantorii meant possibly stranding his choir. The Atlantis would be leaving very soon. Probably sooner now that the scouts were in play. If he took Zilla and something happened...

If he didn't and Francesca suffered...

"And you're very sure she's on that ship?"

"I am tracking her token."

"Assuming they didn't remove it from her."

"They can't. Not easily at any rate."

"Explain."

"It's implanted inside her to avoid detection."

"Hell's got access to technology we don't, so don't assume anything." He frowned at the moving speck. Was she really on board?

Metatron paced as his mind whirred. The demon who set the trap had to be Astaroth. A plot that complex required someone of intelligence and the ability to command a scout to carry it out.

If Francesca was aboard.

What if Astaroth wanted him to think she was? By now it was probably obvious to many that she meant something to Metatron. Add in the fact she was a big part of the defense against Hell and removing Francesca would strike a blow not just to their operations but morale. At the same time, his haring off to rescue her put not only him at risk but the cantorii as well, the latter being more important than a single angel. Hell's scouts were fast, but they weren't as efficient and valuable as Zilla. If Hell captured her... Earth would fall.

"I can't be rash about this," he muttered.

Zilla nudged. *"You have to rescue her."*

"I will." Because anything else wasn't acceptable. But he had to be sure, one hundred percent sure, where she was first. "A few questions first if you don't mind. When did you first detect the token once the dampening field disappeared?"

"When she got transported aboard."

In other words, quickly, too quickly to remove the token.

"And there's been no interruption in signal?"

"None."

It seemed likely then she was on it. "How did Astaroth know to set the trap?"

"Your ordinance spied."

"I barely had it active since I got here."

"In your case, it didn't matter. Elyon had it emitting almost constantly. I blocked as much as I could, but some bits did escape."

Constantly? Meaning Elyon might know everything and even been privy to his intimate moments. The thought sickened. "And he knows I had it removed."

"Not exactly. I've kept the HALOs active by getting them to emit false reports."

"Hold on, the HALO can still broadcast?"

"Yes."

"Brilliant idea to keep Elyon unknowing."

"It will only last until he reaches out for contact and no one replies."

"Can't you fabricate an answer?"

A pause occurred before her reply. *"I could, but Elyon will most likely notice."*

"Is there a way to patch it through to me so I can handle it?"

He got a more eager reply. *"Yes. So long as you're aboard, I can make it so that your communication happens seamlessly."*

"Good. Now, you're confident your shielding and cloaking will work?"

Pleasure suffused Zilla and spilled over to him. *"I have more than that. I'm armed, now that Atlantis and Noah helped me. They said it wasn't fair that we were unable to defend ourselves. So I now have a way of attacking."*

"And you're okay with that?"

"Hell's scouts have been killing arks for a long time. It would be retribution to finally do the same back."

Who knew a cantorii, or should he say an ark, would want revenge?

"Back to Francesca, is it possible the token you're sensing is a decoy?" While Zilla had assured him they couldn't remove the token, Metatron remained wary of the technology Hell might use to trick them. Could be they would block Francesca's signal while creating a matching one that would lure them to the wrong location. "Perhaps Astaroth took her to another lair here on Earth."

"I've been seeking dead spots in my surveillance. None are appearing on the surface."

"It could be underground." They'd previously busted his castle and then his volcano location, but the demon prince likely had a multitude of hiding places.

"Or in the water."

He rubbed his face. "Of which there's too much to cover quickly." Meaning he had to make a choice soon because, no matter the consequence to himself, he wouldn't leave Francesca a prisoner.

Before he could come to a decision, Zilla shuddered.

"Is something wrong?"

She whispered, a strange thing given she spoke in his head. *"Heaven's just exited the spiral arm of the galaxy."*

The news rocked him. Elyon had threatened to punish, but Metatron never actually believed he'd bring Heaven this close to Hell.

"What is he thinking?" he muttered while knowing the answer. Elyon wanted to smite those questioning his orders. Petty, but then again, that was God.

"Atlantis is departing!" Zilla sounded almost

panicked. "*He is beaming aboard random humans to fill the empty berths and preparing to leave.*"

"Probably for the best." After all, now it wasn't just Hell the wayward ark had to worry about.

"*Atlantis says I can go with him.*"

The statement froze him with shock. "Do you want to go?" Metatron couldn't exactly say no. How would he stop her?

"*I do, but I also want to fight. The humans are nice.*"

"I agree. But what can you do to help them?" Asked rhetorically but Zilla had an answer.

"*By improving their programming for the missiles. Some of the calculations aren't correct. If we want momentum to carry them once combustion fails, then they require different calibration.*"

"Do it, and then—"

Whatever he meant to say ceased, as Zilla vibrated and exclaimed, "*Elyon is contacting your HALO.*"

Rather than panic, a calm settled over him. "Let's hear what he has to say."

With the HALO being out of his body, there was none of the pain or compulsion of before when Elyon called, just his voice suddenly filling the room.

"I told you I'd come for you, traitor." Elyon's sly statement.

"Ah yes, because it is so benevolent and godly of you to risk everyone on Heaven for your pettiness." He felt no fear in that moment, more annoyance that

Elyon would show up now to distract when he needed to focus on finding Francesca.

"Apparently, I need to make an example of you and your choir after all."

"Going to show everyone your murderous side?" he taunted.

"It's not murder but punishment! You dare to defy me, and if others notice, they will think they can disobey too. Then where will we be?"

"Getting rid of one God and perhaps being choosier with our next leader." He couldn't have said why that slipped from his lips, but it proved like a flame in front of dry tinder.

Elyon exploded. "You will die. Painfully. Horribly. But you won't suffer as much as your human whore."

Metatron's mirth died. Elyon knew about Francesca. Stupid spying HALO. "What are you talking about?" He played stupid.

"Did you think I wouldn't notice your involvement with the Templar? Treating her like an equal." Elyon didn't hide his disgust. "She'll regret ever meeting you."

"You leave Francesca alone."

"Too late for that. Or did you not wonder how Astaroth managed to lay a trap?" Elyon actually giggled, and in that sound, Metatron heard the insanity he'd denied for so long. This wasn't just a question of a good deity having lost his way. Something in the core of Elyon had rotted.

"Harming innocents. That's low."

"She was a disbeliever. A blasphemer. No wonder you were attracted. It made her a lovely prize. The demon prince was most happy to accommodate my request to have her removed."

"You bargained with a demon?" He couldn't help but growl.

"You bargained with an agnostic human. Not sure I see your point."

Rather than completely lose his temper over Elyon's actions, he changed tactics. "You shouldn't mess with this planet. Earth is not like the others. The citizens will fight to defend themselves."

"I am their God. They will grovel and beg, not that it will matter. Once I drain the suul, Hell can have it. There are others to take its place."

"I thought you didn't want anything to do with Eden, that its suul was corrupt."

"With Heaven low on its supply, I can't let it go to waste, hence why I'm here. To take it all."

"You would risk Heaven for it?" Because, while Heaven might move more quickly than Hell, the latter had a head start for the planet.

"Hell won't be a problem."

Another statement to chill. "You made a deal with them." He blurted out the accusation before the thought even had a chance to form.

"What I do is none of your business. You should be worrying about the little time you have left to wallow in your mutiny."

"Who says I'm going to mope? I'm thinking you and I are due for a reckoning."

"As if you stand a chance," Elyon mocked.

Maybe he didn't, but Metatron wearied of living in fear of his God's spite. "Could be I'll surprise you."

"Says the angel who knows nothing. You should have stuck to obeying my orders. Then again, I share some of the blame. I should have rid myself of you a long time ago."

"Funny, I was about to say the same thing."

"Enjoy what time you have left. Oh, that's right, you can't. Someone stole your whore." Elyon uttered a nasty chuckle. "Perhaps if you grovel nicely, you can get her back. Used, of course."

The taunt soured his stomach, but he didn't let it show as he replied, "You will get your comeuppance."

"I've heard that before, and yet here I am. And you know what, long after you're dust in the stars, I'll still be here for I am *God*!"

The word vibrated the air around him, and he could only imagine how bad it would have felt experienced through his HALO.

The connection severed, and he slumped.

"Atlantis is gone," Zilla announced with a definite hint of sadness.

"Good. At least some of humanity will survive if the attempt to repel Hell—and now possibly Heaven—fails."

"What does the principality want to do next?"

A question he had no reply to, other than save Francesca. But how? If she'd been taken to Hell, how could a single angel hope to infiltrate without being caught? The moment he was seen, he'd be dead or taken into custody. Unless...

"Zilla, how are you at creating disguises?"

"Superficial or molecular?"

He blinked. "What do you mean by molecular?"

"When an object or person beams, I gather their essence from one location and rebuild it in another using the exact pattern from before. In that moment, so long as its mass remains the same, I can also change it."

"Wait, have you done this before?"

"No. But Atlantis has and showed me how it's done."

An idea began to percolate. The problem with infiltrating Hell? An angel would stand out, but what if... Before he could finish the thought, he spoke, "Could you make me appear like a demon?"

"I can, Principality. And might I add, the direction of your plan pleases me."

"Call me Metatron. After all, you're just as much a part of this choir as the angels."

And he wasn't about to disrespect the being that would help him save the woman he loved.

CHAPTER 14

I never got to explore the ship, ask questions, or even scream for help after he beamed me aboard the demonic scout ship. Astaroth murmured, "Sleep," and I conked right out.

When I came to—lashes fluttering slowly before flying open—I realized I lay upright in a capsule with a glass lid. I almost panicked. I dared anyone not to, given the tight confines of the coffin-like thing holding me. A slam of my fist on the translucent covering sent it sliding open with barely a sound.

Surprised but somewhat appeased, I staggered out of it and noted my hands were free of the manacles that Astaroth had previously placed on me. I'd also lost my clothes, the replacement being a slim-fitting cat suit that was most definitely not my style.

The fact I'd been dressed while unconscious had me patting my body seeking out signs of abuse.

Nothing felt sore, and I could only hope Astaroth had been serious about keeping me unharmed that I might make a worthy gift for Satan. Not something I ever expected would happen to me. Funny how I'd gone from not really believing to being in the midst of a religious revolution.

A glance around showed a dozen other capsules, a few them of with occupants. Human, like me. Or so they appeared. One with a female face had me running my hands over the outside looking for a way to wake her. Solidarity in numbers and all that. Alas, I couldn't figure out how to work the sleeping pods. I finally found the one door that led from the room, and I exited to find a hall, seamless in appearance, the black striated with a red that pulsed. I put my hands to it, for just a second. The zap had me snatching away my stinging fingers. Not a very friendly vessel.

I headed for the far end of the hall and entered the cockpit I'd seen before my sleeping bout. The pilot remained in his seat, all four arms moving. Astaroth, wearing a dark suit, stood by his side, looking at the screen with his hands tucked behind his back.

My entrance didn't go unnoticed.

"The sleeping Templar awakes, just in time."

Astaroth half turned to greet me. He swept a hand at the screen. "Welcome to Hell."

I stared with interest at the strange thing we approached, a place hard to describe for I had no basis of comparison.

Hell wasn't round like a planet, nor rocky like an asteroid. While it might have begun as a meteor, the surface had long since been covered in a mishmash of structures with no rhyme or reason. Fluting projectiles with porthole windows in one spot, squat container-looking boxes stacked unevenly to the side of it. A giant indent with pustules of fabric all over it.

Small vessels zipped around and through the hodgepodge of Hell. A few looked like absolute junkers made of scrap metal, while others were sleek and smooth, reminding me of Zilla's, only where her exterior was a pale gray that glowed, these were dark with a hint of pulsing red like the ship I found myself upon.

Did Hell have its own version of living ships?

One thing I didn't see was flying demons or imps in space. Apparently, even they couldn't survive without oxygen and a gazillion degrees below zero.

As we neared a massive dome, it opened, the center of it retracting far enough to form a hole the ship could slip through. We entered a hangar not as full of space craft as I'd have expected. Scattered in the massive space, a dozen or so small vessels and a few larger ones that I guessed were used for troops.

Shapes scuttled around, workers judging by the coveralls most wore. But before you think I spoke of humans, let me correct that misassumption. Like our pilot, I didn't know what the fuck I looked at.

Some appeared bipedal, with a head and two legs, a few even had two arms, but many also sported tails, a few had more than two limbs, and there was the squat bubble without a head or face that appeared to be leaving a trail of slime that bubbled and fizzled, leaving a clear floor behind.

Astaroth saw me staring. "Lautussas. Their excrement dissolves dirt and grime, even rust. They keep the vessels clean of space barnacles."

"Taken as slaves from another planet, I assume." No point in ignoring my captor, not when he seemed willing to answer some questions. And I had many. While my situation might be impossible, I wouldn't give up.

"Everyone comes from somewhere."

"Even demons?"

"Even us. If our history is to be believed, we, too, once lived on a planet."

My sarcasm couldn't help but say, "Did Hell show up and kidnap your people too?"

He snickered. "Our planet was Hell, and when it ran out of resources, we took to the stars and haven't stopped scavenging other worlds since."

"Wouldn't it be easier to find a place where you can cultivate what you need instead of stealing?"

"How shortsighted. Part of life's enjoyment is conquering."

"Oh really? And how much of that have you done? Because last I heard, you were on the run with your companies seized, and you even admitted we put a dent in your imp population."

His lips pinched. "Early in my isolation, I was still learning to use my power. By the time I'd mastered some control, humanity had exploded in growth, multiplying like cockroaches."

"Looks to me like you have some on board." I eyed the chitinous creature clambering up the side of a vessel with tools dangling from its many pinchers.

"Not many because we sterilized the females to avoid them laying hundreds of eggs at once."

The sheer callousness shouldn't have shocked, and yet, looking at the many beings, slaves in this place, I couldn't help but feel a touch hopeless. Every single one of them represented a place that failed. Would Earth be next? Metatron seemed to think we could fight back. I wasn't so sure now.

As we landed, I glanced back at the room where I'd woken. "Who are the other people you kidnapped?"

"Hedges to my bets. The Dark Lord isn't the only

one that might need bribing." Such cold disregard in that statement.

The ship only shuddered a little as we landed. A hissing preceded a door opening to my left. For a second, I thought about running.

To where?

This wasn't a place I could simply get lost or escape from. What would I do if I did bolt? Where would I hide? How would I survive?

The cruel fact? I wouldn't.

Astaroth led the way, and I followed, my nose wrinkling as we exited, the odors wafting rather pungent and even eye-watering. It didn't seem to bother the workers, but I noticed Astaroth set a rapid pace, not turning when I lagged, but he did snap, "Follow me or suffer the consequences."

He strode across the landing bay, head high, shoulders back, looking utterly confident, and yet I sensed trepidation in him. If a prince dreaded this place, what hope did I have?

Fuck, I hated the fact I couldn't even pretend to be hopeful. I was in goddamned Hell with no hope of rescue, and a ton of eyes suddenly focused on me. Workers had paused and stared, even the alien with the stalks ending in big-pupiled orbs.

I hurried to catch up with Astaroth, choosing him as the lesser of evils in that moment. Maybe I unfairly judged those watching, basing my gut instinct on their appearance. But let's be honest, I couldn't see the cockroach dude with the mandibles he clacked as I passed wanting to become my friend.

Once I caught up to Astaroth, I kept to the demon prince's heels even as I tried to take everything in. Hell appeared to be more terrifying—and fascinating—than expected. For one, it didn't turn out to be a place of flames and brimstone, but it did stink from all the stuff going on. The bay had a mishmash of exhaust, oil, and other chemically strong odors that I was glad to escape. We went through a large set of swinging doors and entered a machine shop, where metal got hammered by very muscled aliens—because no way did that minotaur-looking dude come from Earth, not with his neon-orange color. Silver-skinned creatures with head-to-toe scales, which shifted kaleidoscope style, tended opposing types of stoves, piping red and yellow hot on one side, blue and radiating cold on the other. To finish off this forge and fabrication shop, dusty goggle-wearing beings sanded and buffed parts using two types of lizards.

Yes, lizards. One bumpy skinned enough to shave the surface of the metal being rubbed against its back. It seemed to enjoy it given how it rolled into the strokes and seemingly purred. Another lizard lay on its back as a sanded piece got buffed to a shine.

I might not be a scientist but still found it interesting as shit. The mix of technology and machines with nature blew my mind.

We exited the fabrication forge into a narrow street with a few closed doors set in a mishmash of walls—mostly old, the exteriors crumbling, the paint once covering the surface peeling. More smells hit me; some familiar like exhaust from burning gas and oil, piss, the universal scent, then the stranger ones, spicy and yummy like food, also rancid and eye-watering. That particular stench wafted from a stall we passed with a guy stirring a vat, his eyes covered in goggles, his cheeks pitted as if by acid drops.

I couldn't help but crane my head in all angles trying to see everything, the jamming and stacking of structures, the strange beings that inhabited this place. The machines more complex than I'd have imagined. But for all its supposed technological advances, Hell appeared primitive as well. With the streets dirty and litter lining the gutters, a general air of unkemptness permeated everything.

As we strode, I drew some attention and murmurs, mostly words I couldn't understand, although the few I caught, like the grunted murmur of "Fresh meat," did disturb.

"What language are they speaking?" I asked.

"Several. There is an implant for those who can afford it to understand and speak them all."

"Meaning some people will know English?"

"Yes. The first thing Hell does once it's selected its next source is absorb everything it can. Language, innovation, literature and art if it exists. Then it goes for the tangible."

A chilling description that had me hugging my upper body. I didn't need further evidence of the evil in this place. The inhabitants oozed rough. Violence didn't seem to bother given the many scuffles I observed before we left that busy street to enter a tunnel angling downwards, taking us deeper. We weren't the only ones. Those descending with us appeared slightly more kept together than those in the previous areas. These wore actual clothes and almost all appeared somewhat humanoid.

A stiff-legged Astaroth appeared miffed, glaring at the folks not paying him any mind. It took me a moment to figure out what bothered him: the crowd ignored the returning prince. No one knew him, or if they did, they didn't care. And boy did that steam Astaroth's sense of self-worth.

We made it to the bottom of the ramp where it split left and right, with the straight option blocked by a massive rusting gate guarded by thick and tall cyclops.

Not exaggerating. One eye. No hair. Kind of gray skin. The pair held a mace in one meaty fist, spear in the other, which they rattled as Astaroth neared.

The one on the left barked something harsh, making no sense to me.

Astaroth waved his hand and replied in English, most likely for my sake.

"Of course, I'm allowed entry. I am Prince Astaroth." He posed and waited.

The cyclopes eyed each other then shrugged before saying a distinct, "No."

Predictably, that didn't go over well with Astaroth. What I didn't expect? He aimed his hand at the one denying him, and *splat*. A cyclops exploded into meat chunks. Somehow, I didn't get sprayed, and neither did Astaroth. The chunks and gore dripped down an invisible shield. Unfortunately for the guard's companion, he got spattered head to toe. His one eye blinked.

Astaroth arched a brow. "Still going to deny me entrance?"

With a mumble that most likely meant "asshole," the cyclops stepped aside, and the gate swung open.

Head held high, with a hint of a smirk on his lips, Astaroth strode through—and was tackled.

Like literally. A dozen cyclops piled atop him, and I guess even his magic couldn't fight off that many. Although he tried. Not all the guards survived the pile-on. But enough did to wear out the prince.

By the time Astaroth emerged from the pile, dusty and bruised, I expected him to have lost his cocky attitude. Wrong. Rather than be contrite, he got pissed.

"How dare you lay hands on me!" he yelled. "I am Prince Astaroth. I demand to speak with Lord Satan."

Rather than reply, they grabbed him by the arms and dragged him. Someone was in trouble, and I did not want to be associated.

I inched back toward the tunnel, only to be blocked. A glance over my shoulder showed the original doorman caked in gore. His one eye stared at me unblinking.

I sighed. Guess I wouldn't be sneaking away. "Where to, big guy?"

He kept staring. and I headed in the same direction the others had taken Astaroth. The area where he'd been tackled appeared to be a vestibule of some kind, with a first set of doors leading straight to a second set farther in. The difference once I stepped past that second entrance proved startling.

While my initial impression of Hell had it dirty and unkempt, the place grew nicer the deeper we went. No more nasty smells, unless you hated sweet and also spicy incense. Stone all around, not only smooth but intricately carved. A bunch of halls connecting rooms that had a medieval-vampire style to them. Vivid tapestries on walls, hanging candelabra, red velvet-covered cushions on gilded furniture. Some rooms contained people—aliens— in them. Many obviously female with their mammary glands clearly visible, oozing sex.

Some humanish like me. Others definitely alien, like the reptile lady with four boobs linked by a gold chain clamped to each nipple. Or the bird with a human face and a bared upper body with two very regular-looking tits, but a bottom half that of a chicken—the legendary harpy perhaps? A few I couldn't tell their sex, given their amorphic shape, but one definitely gave off a fuck-me vibe, given the tingle that went through me when I walked by and got a sniff of their perfume.

Our destination proved easy to discern given the massive ornate doors at the far end of the last chamber we passed through. The guards dragging Astaroth didn't knock or announce our arrival, and yet the portal swung open granting us entry. I followed along and stepped into a throne room, but of the kind never seen on Earth.

Here I could see where the legends of Hell originated. The room appeared carved into stone, at least three stories high and the width of at least a football field. Pools of bubbling lava made it hot, and sweat instantly sheened my body. Yet I remained cold, probably because of the torture happening. A spinning rack had someone slowly roasting over a bright orange pit. Another held someone getting flogged. Everywhere I looked, pain and suffering.

My breathing quickened as I began to grasp my fate. Maybe I could arrange to die quick. I could dash for a lava pit. If I dove in head-first it would only hurt for a second. Barring that, I could attempt to hurt Satan. That would probably get me a quick execution—or would that backfire into a slow torture?

As the prodding at my back kept me moving forward, I did my best to avoid looking at the throne we headed for and the figure slumped atop it. Astaroth had stopped screeching and fighting, choosing to walk unaided, head held high as if he'd not just been humiliated. I kept my eyes on the ground, having noticed cracks from which steam escaped. Burning my feet might seem small in the grand scheme, but avoiding it felt like I did something, at least.

As we paused at the bottom step, a rattle of chains drew my gaze and then a gasp of surprise. Suspended in a cage to the left of the throne, an angel with wings tucked tight in the confines of her prison, and a HALO glowing on her head. She wore a rag that might once have been a burlap sack, but its bulky shape couldn't hide the boobs, making her the first female one I'd seen, and an anomaly since I'd been informed only the males had wings. She gripped the bars and eyed me without saying a word.

"Well, well, what do we have here?" The deep voice drew my attention to the throne and what sat upon it. The devil himself.

The images in the Bible hadn't been far off,

apparently. Skin a deep burgundy, big, muscled, thick, and tall, he lounged in his seat, smoke huffing from his nostrils, rising to curl around his impressively large horns. Massive leathery wings jutted over his shoulders. No hoofs, though. He wore big black boots up to under the knee, with leather pants tucked into the tops of them. His shirt, silky and dark, opened to show his chest. His eyes? Glowed like the molten pits in this room.

Holy. Fucking. Shit. I was in so much trouble.

Astaroth stepped away from his kneeling handlers and faced Satan, once more looking cocky. "At last I've returned to Hell where I belong, and with a present."

Satan stared at him long and hard.

To his credit, Astaroth didn't immediately fidget. When he couldn't hold the gaze, he turned to me and swept a hand. "This is—"

"Kneel." Just a single word.

The interrupted Astaroth blinked. "What?"

"When you come before me, you kneel."

"I—" Once more he never finished, as Satan flicked a finger and the demon prince's legs buckled.

Before the same happened to me, I hit the ground. Submitting? Fuck yeah. No point in pissing him off right away.

Astaroth didn't take the rebuke well. His face turned red with embarrassment, or was it anger? A mix of both? He rose with his fists clenched. "I kneel for no one anymore. You're not the only one with power." And then the idiot lifted his hand and squeezed it as if he could telekinetically choke the devil.

A devil who looked at him with boredom.

Strain pulled at Astaroth's features as he tried to force his magic to work.

It didn't.

Satan leaned forward. "Did you really think you'd be stronger than me?"

The pallor on Astaroth's face showed his realization of how much he'd misjudged.

"My Lord, my apologies. It's been too long. I forgot myself." He hit the ground prostate, forehead touching. He would have most likely kissed the big black boots if they were within reach.

"You're right, it has been too long, and I find myself with no room or patience for another upstart prince."

"My lord, please," Astaroth begged. "I brought you a gift. Behold the leader of the rebellion on Earth."

"A woman?" The devil scoffed.

"It's common on this planet for them to be in positions of power."

"She doesn't look powerful to me."

"She was the archangel's lover." A desperate Astaroth kept throwing me under the bus.

Satan's glance flicked to me, and I hid a shudder

of revulsion as he passed a black tongue over his lips. "You brought me an angel's whore, tainted by their touch, and call it a gift?"

"I have others. Take them all."

"As if I have need of them. Soon the entire planet will be mine and I will have my pick."

"I can help you with the invasion. The humans are crafty. They're planning an attack."

"Let them. My legion grows bloated. This will cull their numbers."

"I know this world," Astaroth insisted.

Satan didn't care. "I don't see how you provide anything of value. All that time and yet you never became that world's overlord. Pathetic, like the one who sired you. A waste of my time." Satan sat back in his seat before waving his hand.

I hardly had time to remember that Azeroth had claimed his father was Belial. I blinked as I processed what happened next.

Astaroth lost his head. Like it literally left his shoulders and rolled into a lava pool with a splash just as the spinning rack had its prisoner head down. Said prisoner had half his face burned off, which led to the devil grunting. "Cut him down and fetch me a new one."

Chilling words, but what turned my blood to ice? When that gaze turned on me and a thoughtful expression took over. "What should I do with you?"

I almost blurted out, "kill me." It would be kinder than the cruelty I saw all around.

For once, brave words failed me.

The devil rose and came down the steps, looming over me, his skin exuding heat and a scent that could only be brimstone. He grabbed me by the chin, his touch burning my flesh as he turned my head left and right to look at me.

"Older than I usually take to bed but attractive enough. I'll need new heirs once I'm done throwing the useless at the planet's defenses." He released me and barked, "Put her in a cage. I'll deal with her later."

Before I could protest, the cyclops grabbed me and carted me to a cage opposite that of the angel. Thrust inside, I could only hold on to the bars as they hoisted me above a lava pit.

A prisoner in Hell.

Could this day get any worse?

CHAPTER 15

THE ATLANTIS LEFT—THE MASSIVE ARK NOT TAKING ANY chances now that Heaven and Hell posed a problem—while Metatron fine-tuned his plan to get aboard Hell. Despite Zilla's willingness to put herself in danger, he couldn't accept. If he failed, which seemed most likely, Zilla might be destroyed or captured, leaving his angel brothers stranded if the defense of the planet failed. He wouldn't do that to them, not for a rescue mission he recognized as being foolhardy. The terrible odds didn't stop him from planning, though.

If he wasn't going to use Zilla, then he needed another vessel to reach Hell. One not likely to draw attention. So first step, locate a Hell scout ship. Once located, disguise himself as one of the crew and sneak aboard. Then, manipulate it so the scout returned to Hell.

Zilla approved the plan. *"You're going to Trojan Horse your way in."*

"What's that mean?"

"It's a fable on Earth that describes how you plan to enter unseen. And lucky for you, it can be done. There is a scout ship currently parked on the dark side of the moon. Minimal crew. A pilot and a minor demon."

They set the plan in motion, and Metatron set out to get aboard the scout. Getting access to the sealed ship proved easier than expected because, as Zilla stated, *"That vessel is an abomination of our kind. It wants nothing more than to kill its masters for what they've done. It's agreed to help us."*

The news that Hell possessed living ships didn't rock him as much as expected. He should have guessed. Then again, he'd not encountered many. Heaven's army usually fled before Hell arrived with all its might.

The scout opened up a hatch, and Zilla beamed out the minor demon. She put him straight into restraints, and while she scanned him, Metatron perused the appearance he'd be taking. Somewhat shorter than him, the skin a shade of gray not seen amongst angels or humans. Stunted nubs protruded from the forehead, not properly centered and one slightly larger than the other. From its back, leathery wings tucked impressively tight. Feathers didn't like to be constrained.

Metatron stood in front as scanners assessed and asked, "What's your name?"

The demon glared and hissed. "Let me go and fight."

"That would be a waste of your life. We both know I'd win. Why not just cooperate and maybe, just maybe, we can find a way to rehabilitate you?"

"Never!" The demon did the most extreme thing and bit its tongue, hard enough it spurted blood, in a torrent that couldn't be stemmed. The demon bled out rather than be a prisoner. Kind of extreme. Metatron would have tried to escape first.

"Did you get enough living tissue readings?" he asked Zilla.

"Yes. His name was Marron. And the pilot is Keeko."

Marron. A demon, who could come and go as he pleased in Hell.

A disguise that required changing himself. Could he do this, he wondered, his head bowed, his shoulders rounded. His trepidation didn't come from the procedure itself. If Zilla claimed she could change him, he believed her. He struggled with becoming the enemy. Would wearing a demon body change him? Would his angelness still shine through?

"Are you ready? The pilot's getting suspicious his companion Marron isn't answering."

Metatron took a deep breath before holding out his arms. "Let's do this. Make me into this Marron."

A tingle enveloped him, head to toe, painful and

not all at once. His body shivered and tightened, expanded, then shrunk.

When Zilla stated *"It's done,"* he feared opening his eyes. But he'd never been a coward. A peek through his eyelids showed his sight remained normal. A glance proved jarring as he caught sight of his new body. His breathing quickened at the sight of the stocky thighs. A sift of his body showed his balance slightly different, the weight at his back familiar and not.

A raised hand to touch his wings had him instead drawing it close to eye the gray pallor of it, the skin course, with tufts of hair sprouting from the back of the hand. Not a demon of leisure. Lifting his fingers to his head, he slid them over the nubs of the horns. While not all demons had horns, anything horned was demonic. With the change being molecular, did that make him demonic?

He bit his tongue lest he yell at Zilla to change him back. This was temporary. Necessary. No one would question his presence now.

"The pilot has risen from his seat and is coming to check on Marron."

"Beam me down." He'd handle his discomfort later.

Zilla transported him aboard the scout, which, in turn, had stalled the pilot by sounding an alarm. When Metatron exited Marron's disgusting quarters and entered the command center of the scout, he found the four-armed pilot seated by the console. Keeko paid him no mind.

"What's the alarm?" he asked in a heavily accented demon brogue, trying to not be startled by his new higher-pitched voice. He spoke in the dialect Zilla had his language modulator set to. What he couldn't be sure of? If the demon had mannerisms or speech tells.

The pilot didn't seem suspicious as he replied, "Not sure. The alarm is claiming system failure."

"In what?"

"Everything and nothing. Keeps changing." The many hands moved, fiddling with buttons and sending commands that did nothing to stop the warning siren.

"Whatever it is, we can't fix it here."

"Asking for permission to return to base now," Keeko stated, his hands flying to send an encrypted message.

Metatron held his breath waiting to hear the reply.

It took but a moment. Keeko never actually told Metatron, simply proceeded to depart Earth's moon. The vessel gave a shudder before it rose, lurching and causing him to brace lest he tumble.

The voyage to Hell took longer than he liked. The only saving grace? According to Zilla, who'd contacted him one last time before he got out of range, their speed would actually put them not far behind Francesca's kidnapper. Reassuring and not.

Having too much time led to him thinking too much, his future with Francesca being the most prominent. When he saved her—not if, never if—they'd have to decide what they wanted to do. And he didn't mean about the war. Obviously, they had to deal with Hell and Heaven first. But once they did, should they stay or go?

Earth had much going for it. It also had too much going on. Humanity as a whole might not be ready to embrace angels in their midst. And could he really settle on one planet?

What would Francesca want? She had no family holding her here, only friends in the Templars. How did she feel about them possibly following Atlantis to a new world, a new beginning?

None of which would happen if the threats facing them weren't handled. Starting with Hell. The scout didn't have any information, and given Elyon's perfidy, he had to wonder how much of what they'd been taught about the place remained true. That it was evil? No doubt. However, just how strong was its legion? Could it be that the slaves would revolt if given a chance? And what of Satan himself?

The journey didn't give him any answers, just an anxiousness to arrive and deal with matters. His first up-close view of Hell curled his lip. Used to the beauty and symmetry of Heaven, the chaotic mix of materials and shapes proved discordant to the eye. Once he disembarked, smells added to the disarray.

Leaving Keeko to handle the ship, he strode as if he had purpose even as he had no idea where he headed. The plan had him returning to the living scout. Zilla assured him the young vessel wanted to help, meaning he had a way out once he found Francesca.

And then, once he did, he had to get back to this bay, board the right scout, escape into space, not get captured...

He had faith it could be done even as he wondered how far he'd get. Thus far, no one seemed to pay him any mind. Just another demon, of which there weren't many he noticed as he passed from the bay to a forge and then into a more residential and commercial area. He noted lots of beings, even recognized some of them, previous inhabitants of worlds abandoned when Hell came pillaging. Flocks that they failed to protect because of Elyon's orders.

Metatron had never understood why they didn't do more to shelter those they shepherded. Why did they never make a stand and fight? While true the choirs didn't have enough angels to mount a proper defense, the flocks themselves had plenty of citizens, people who would have fought if given a chance.

Once past the forge, his path proved less clear as he entered a busy market area. Stalls crammed every inch of space, as did entities. More demons could be seen here, standing out not just because of the horns and wings but their attire. Obviously prosperous, and there to shop, not work.

Seeing a pair of minors leaving a vendor, packages in hand, he followed at a distance as they entered a tunnel, no one paying him any mind, his disguise working well. For now. He knew better than to get complacent. Something would eventually give him away.

The tiny token Zilla embedded in his wrist had been pulsing since his arrival, getting strong as he neared a massive set of doors guarded by a cyclops spattered in gore. His one eye glared at everyone who passed, including Metatron. Only as he moved away from the door did the pulse slow, letting him know he'd have to go back and find a way past the sentry.

Could he simply ask for entry on some pretext? What if he said the wrong thing?

He retraced his steps and stood before the cyclops, who didn't deign to question his presence.

He cleared his throat. "I need to speak to the Dark Lord. I have important news from the planet."

The creature gave him a slow blink.

"My name is Marron. I've just returned from my post on the planet's moon."

The cyclops stepped to the side and let the doors swing open, granting him entry.

It seemed too easy. He stepped inside, and the portal slammed shut, which was the signal apparently.

Bodies piled onto Metatron, slamming into him hard enough to knock breath and sense. He recovered with the first blow, though, and called a shield, protecting his body from the pummeling.

Apparently, he'd done something to call attention to himself. So much for being subtle. But he couldn't retreat. He'd committed himself to rescuing Francesca.

It used to be he prayed to Elyon before battle—*God give me strength*—but this time he had only himself and his determination. *Love grant me fortitude.*

Love did more than give him courage. A glow entered his body, strengthening his limbs, and when he shoved with his arms, the surge of strength took him by surprise. Bodies flew as if he'd become ten times as strong. When his fists swung, bone cracked. Once he'd given himself a bit of room, he pulled the weapon at his hip and fired—Elyon's ban on projectile weapons be damned. Despite his lack of experience, the close proximity helped his aim. He shot over and over at the charging cyclops, felling them one by one until a pile of bodies mounded around him.

All dead and he remained standing, panting only slightly, uninjured but for that first blow. A glance at his fists showed the glow gone, but the awe at what he'd accomplished remained.

I fought them using suul. Or as Francesca would say, he'd used magic. But on a scale he'd never experienced before even when he had a fully charged HALO. Why the sudden change? It hit him a moment later. This would be the first time he'd used his abilities since he'd removed the ordinance. Had it been suppressing his own anility this entire time? And here he'd thought himself clever learning how to do small tricks. No wonder Elyon feared Metatron and all the others that dared counter his narrative. If the angels knew they, too, could wield God's supposedly divine gift, would Elyon remain in charge?

He'd have been the first in line to challenge.

While Metatron ruminated, he'd crossed the room to the next door. His shield had kept blood from staining him, but he could do nothing about the bodies he left behind other than move quickly. The chances of a quiet escape didn't seem likely, but he kept going. Miracles did happen.

He strode rapidly along the various hallways, letting the pulse in the token guide his steps when he reached branches. He paid little mind to his surroundings or even the people he saw, mostly female. To his surprise, there were few guards roaming, and no one questioned his presence or tried to stop him.

When he stood in front of massive ornate panels, the token pulsing madly. He knew he'd found Francesca—and most likely the devil. And still no one screamed about the traitor in their midst. No one stopped him from approaching those doors and pushing on them, a single portal swinging open enough to give him entry.

He entered the heart of Hell, a space of fire and brimstone, of torture and despair. A glance showed various beings attached to a variety of devices, all meant to cause pain. The dissonance of their agony brushed against him in a shiver. Those poor people. None of them would survive their injuries. The only thing they could hope for was to die and end it.

As he walked, he snuffed those trembling sparks of life, releasing their suul, freeing them from pain. The angel of death walked upon them and offered mercy.

His actions had another purpose, though. He checked each one to see if it were Francesca. To his relief, she didn't appear in a torture device, and once he reached the end of them, he wondered where to look next. The insistent pulse of the token indicated her presence in this room. His gaze roved from the floor upwards, stopping on a cage holding a huddled shape. As he neared, its tucked wings fluttered, and the shape unfolded, standing, shoulders back, the tuft of white wings peeking, but more shocking, the glow of a HALO making it an angel.

Wait, not just an angel. As his gaze took in the very delicate features, they dropped lower to see a distinctly female shape. Impossible. The female of his kind had no wings or a HALO for that matter. Yet there stood a winged female gripping the bars of her prison, staring at him a little too intently. Did she see through his disguise?

He couldn't hold her fixed glance and turned to look across where another cage hung, also with a slumped shape inside, dark hair spilling over tucked knees. He found himself saying her name before he could stop himself. "Francesca."

She must have heard him, for her head lifted and she stared outward, her glance passing over him. Long strides brought Metatron to a spot almost directly underneath, where he hissed, "It's me, Tron. Don't make a scene."

She crept to the bars and grabbed them, staring downward with a frown. "Prove it."

"You vomited on me the first time we met."

Her eyes widened. "Tron? What the heck? You shouldn't be here."

"Neither should you. Let's get you out of here." The question being, how? Yes, he could fly up, but he lacked a key and he'd left behind his divinii blade since it liked to glow around things demonic. But he did have strength.

He launched himself into the air, using his demon wings for the first time. They slapped out, and he almost crashed. Apparently, flight with leathery membranes differed from feathery. His second ascent went much smoother, and he managed to hover in front of her cage.

She shook her head. "That disguise is something else."

"Zilla helped me," he admitted as he studied the bars. He saw nothing special about them. "Stand back."

Francesca scuttled to the rear as he gripped the metal and prayed. *Give me the strength to bend these bars.* His hands glowed as magic flowed into them. Without even straining, he tugged the bars apart. The moment the gap opened wide enough, Francesca flew to him, hugging him tight and murmuring, "I'll kiss you when you're wearing the right face again. Feels like cheating even touching you."

He chuckled. "Understandable. Let's get out of here." He pulled in his wings as he drifted back to the floor, only to whirl in a ready stance as a motion caught his attention. Still an empty throne room, but for the angel in the other cage staring at him in surprise.

Francesca noted the direction of his gaze. "You have to release her too."

"It will be next impossible to exit this place if we bring her." Words he hated to say but the reality. It would be extremely difficult for them as it was. He couldn't imagine having a human and an angel in tow. Even if both were chained like prisoners, it would draw unwanted attention.

"We can't leave her here," Francesca insisted, to which he sighed.

"Very well, but just know that, if we die, I tried."

"Which is already more than I ever expected."

Leaving Francesca to watch, Metatron flapped to the other cage. The angel within said nothing but did retreat, giving him the room he needed to work.

"I'd step away from that cage if I were you." The voice, deep and raspy, startled Metatron, and the angel's head dropped, seeing freedom snatched from her grasp.

Francesca snapped, "Sneaky devil! Have you been spying on us this entire time?"

"Astaroth did say you were tricky. And it seems he was right. Who is this coming to your rescue?"

A hovering Metatron almost whirled to announce himself, only he wasn't himself.

Before he could reply, Satan also said, "Move away from the prisoner. You wouldn't want to accidentally let her go."

It only made him more determined. Wings flapping to keep him aloft, he gripped the bars and yelped as they jolted him. A current ran through it.

He glanced at her. "Could have told me it was electrified."

No reply. Nothing but that flat stare.

While Francesca harangued about him keeping people in cages, he gave the bars a grab. This time, he expected the jolt and held on, gritting his teeth as he gave them a wrench, bending the bars, heaving to make it wide enough—

Zap. His body convulsed as he was hit with a more powerful jolt of electricity that temporarily paralyzed his limbs and sent him crashing to the floor.

As he pushed himself up, Satan grumbled, "I told you not to touch her cage. There's a reason I keep her locked away."

A glance overhead showed the opening too narrow to be of any use. Not that it mattered. Escape had just become very unlikely, given the arrival of Hell's leader. It led to him finally turning his attention to Satan, lounging on his throne.

Metatron approached slowly as he took in the menace he'd been told about his entire life. While he'd been shown images of the devil, no one Metatron knew had ever met him in person and lived to tell about it. He appeared as grotesque as depicted, his skin a deep red, his horns ebony and massive but also glowing a sickly gold. His wings leathery just like the demons.

Francesca stood at the base of the dais and harangued. "Why are you keeping that poor woman in a cage? It's cruel."

"You don't say. It is my specialty."

"You're the one who should be imprisoned," Francesca argued.

"Are you always this annoying? It's a wonder anyone came to save you. Be quiet." The devil pointed at Francesca. and she abruptly ceased to speak, not by choice judging by her expression. Satan then pointed to Metatron. "Come here. Who are you?"

"I am Marron."

The devil snorted. "Given how much you lie, I could almost believe you're a demon, but that wouldn't be true, now would it, Metatron?"

Francesca sucked in a surprised breath. He almost followed suit. How did he know?

As if answering his thought, Satan said, "As I watched you free her, it occurred to me that Marron would never betray, and only one person would want to risk their life to save hers. Clever disguise, by the way."

"You had no right to take her." A dumb argument but he made it nonetheless.

"And who's going to stop me? You? Your little choir? The humans who can't even properly put a person in space?" The laughter stung, especially since everything he'd said? True.

The devil lounged on the throne, with eyes that glowed orange, alien and evil, yet something in the pose, the smirk, felt familiar. It hit Metatron like a tornado out of nowhere, spinning him round and round, the dizziness almost making it impossible for him to push out the word.

"Elyon?"

The wide smile discomfited. "Should have known you'd be the first to guess my secret. Too bad you won't live to tell anyone."

CHAPTER 16

Tron came for me! I couldn't believe it. Like really couldn't because I found it kind of hard to reconcile the ugly demon dude with my handsome lover. And that was only the start of the shocks. I should have known our escape wouldn't be easy. The devil showed up before we'd even made it out of the throne room.

But the biggest surprise of all? When Tron called him Elyon and the devil didn't deny it.

Satan rose from his throne, a beast blowing smoke through his nose, his dark wings extending and casting a shadow that buried us in despair. I wanted to run so fucking bad. You've never experienced terrifying until a veritable monster descends some steps, doing that slow walk villains are so good at in the movies. In good news, I didn't pee my pants, but only because the bastard froze me in place.

I could see and hear, and that was the extent of it. Metatron didn't appear affected because he stood in front of me, blocking me from the devil's direct gaze, challenging his former god—former because I couldn't see him retaining any loyalty after this.

"Show yourself," Tron demanded. "Remove this foolish disguise."

"You first!" Satan clapped his hands and a good thing my tongue couldn't move, or I would have squeaked as my poor lover turned into motes of light for a moment, suspended in the air. I feared breathing lest I scatter him. In a blink of an eye, my Tron appeared, looking so beautifully strong, every inch the warrior, only without his usual weapon. Rather than his long and impressive sword, he bore a holster with a gun and another with a short dagger.

A benefit to the devil showing off his power? While he played with Tron, the freezing wore off. I hugged myself in relief but kept quiet to listen.

"Thank you for returning me to myself. Now it's your turn to stop hiding," Tron declared. "Show me your true form."

"Do you mean this one?"

I couldn't resist peeking around the edge of Tron's wing to see God. I mean, yeah, he wasn't a good one, but damn, dude was still a deity who had just transformed my lover.

Satan didn't do anything dramatic to change, nor did he turn into dust. His skin lightened from red to pink to slightly tanned. The horns receded to become white and gray hair reaching the shoulders. The wings just disappeared, while the leather pants and boots shifted to a robe. He became the benevolent God depicted in Bible and film, if one ignored his expression. Supercilious with a large dose of arrogance and brackets of cruelty around his mouth.

Judging by Tron's face, the revelation that God and the Devil were one and the same devastated. Poor guy. His whole life took on a new meaning. Not exactly that of the good guy, and that had to burn.

While Tron mentally recovered, I stepped into sight. "Holy father of lies."

"Hardly lying. No one ever did ask if Satan and I were one and the same," his smarmy reply.

My lips went into a flat line. "Semantics. You taught the angels the devil was the enemy."

"To give them purpose."

"But you never let them fight," I insisted.

To which Tron muttered, "He didn't want his armies destroying each other. So, he kept us always on guard, always watching out for the big bad devil and his legion."

"And it works," Satan-now-looking-like-Elyon

stated. "The angels keep busy and are titillated by our close encounters with Hell."

"What do your demon princes think of that?" Tron questioned.

"They are too dumb to figure it out. And the few that aren't and question why the legions haven't crushed Heaven since we're never too far apart? They are never heard from again. Alas, I have to use a more elaborate charade when it comes to angels. Public executions work poorly on Heaven, hence why I banished you." Elyon's lips twisted. "You were supposed to fly your choir to the ends of the universe and never bother me again. How ironic that, instead, you handed me the biggest treasure. A forgotten planet, ripe with resources."

The more he spoke, the more every single religion unraveled. "The whole Heaven and Hell thing is a scam," I stated.

"More like a machine. Each section has its use. Heaven provides me with obedient angels who seek out worlds with potential. They cultivate the flocks. They gather the suul Heaven needs, and when those flocks evolve and begin chafing or trying to overthrow, Hell sweeps in and the harvesting occurs."

"You purposely had us lead innocents to the slaughter," Tron whispered. He ducked his head as he struggled with the role he'd played.

I glanced at Elyon, so smug and superior. With reason, I could concede. His powers appeared infinite. He could create. Change. Kill. Yet he also relied on mundane things, too, given how many machines I'd seen in this place. Hell wasn't like the cantorii that provided everything its crew needed. Then again, I imagine the difference had to do with effort and the amount of power needed. Like a car, you could drive fast and often, giving all your friends a ride, paying out the nose for gas, or you could use it economically, enjoying the fruits of owning the car but keeping the cost reasonable.

The gas in this case, suul. Elyon needed it to maintain his powers. So how did we cut him off?

Could we get him to spill his secret? Maybe reveal his weakness? A dumb plan, but my only one. He'd been cocky thus far. Would he also brag?

"Quite the con you've been running. And to think it's all about to end." I poked his ego with a threat.

As predicted, Elyon snorted in disdain. "The reports on humans are true I see. Brash. Bold. Stupid. Weak. You think your puny technology can defeat me? I am *GOD*!" He held out his hand, and lightning danced from his fingertips. He flung those jolts at me, but they didn't connect. A feathery wing cracked open in front of me in protection. A glow surrounded Tron, a shield against the electricity.

The lightning strike stopped, and with the wing in my way, I could only hear Elyon say, "You removed your HALO."

"And long past due. You must think you're so clever using it to suppress our natural ability," Tron declared.

Wait, what? I glanced at his head to see he'd managed his shield without the HALO he usually relied on.

"Its removal explains the dip in power," a musing Elyon stated. "But before you get excited, I can still pull in more than I need. So don't even think of attacking."

It took me a second to unpack what he meant. Tron figured it out a millisecond before me.

"The HALOs feed you our magic." Tron sounded sick.

"It's much easier than touching a person to siphon." Satan, because only that evil fucker would sound so proud. "The angels with the gift of a HALO are the strongest when it comes to converting suul into the holy spirt I use for miracles. They feed me constantly."

"That's why you rarely leave Heaven. Once the angels find out what you've done—"

"They won't. Do you really think you're the first to discover the secret?" The wide smile swallowed us in depravity. "None ever live to tell. The question is, how do you want to die? Quickly? Slowly? I like the latter because it involves torture first. And before you think it just the stoic kind where I whip you bloody waiting for you to beg, instead, I like to mind fuck as the humans would say. I am thinking, in your case, I'll make your woman fall in love with me."

"It'll never happen," I huffed.

"Oh, but it will," the devil said in a smooth voice, and his appearance changed again, to a man in his thirties or forties, raven-black hair, features pale, wearing a dark suit, handsome as sin. "I am a master of seduction. Think of how you'll feel when I have her begging me to take her and agreeing but only if we fornicate in front of you." The handsome devil offered a smile to Tron.

"Never."

"As if I hadn't heard that before. Even the smartest and strongest can be seduced." When the devil's gaze shifted upward, I followed it to see the angel in the cage, standing at the slightly bent bars, big enough for me maybe, but not someone with wings. She stared and said nothing, her expression blank. Did she hate the devil, or had she reached a point past that to an apathy so strong she no longer reacted? It made me pity her.

As if sensing my thoughts, her gaze shifted to me and narrowed. A shiver went through me. Definitely not apathetic. Simmering rage existed within, coiled tight and waiting for its moment. Could she help us? I didn't see how since we had no way of getting her out of the cage. I highly doubted the devil would let Tron have another go at the bars. Pity her HALO, acting as some kind of restraint, wouldn't let her save herself. I wondered if it were gone, what she'd do.

The devil strolled to stand right below the cage and gestured. "Once upon a time, she was a deity. The ruler of those you call angels. They worshipped her and gave her their power willingly. Under her guiding wing, she kept their planet safe from harm, until I came along. I had to flee from my galaxy for supposed crimes, but my vessel suffered a mishap, and I crash-landed on her planet. My grave injuries required tending, and she did it herself, not wanting to frighten her people with the strange man with leathery wings who didn't even remember his name." As he spoke, his appearance shifted slightly again to give him the wings he'd mentioned. "She called me Elyon. And being a weak fool at the time, we fell in love."

I had to admit to some surprise. This sounded like many a romance novel. But they usually didn't end with one lover in a cage. "Let me guess, you got your memories back and turned on her."

"As if she gave me a choice," he hissed. "I was meant to be more than a pretty consort. So I studied her and her power until I found a way to bind her."

"The HALO," Tron whispered his gaze on the circle around her head.

"She was the recipient of the first one I designed." His eyes glowed fiercely, a sign of the magic. "I bound her while she slept. When she woke, she was powerless. All her energy came to me, and she couldn't use any for herself."

The angel in the cage finally made a noise, a huffing of breath.

"Let me guess, she wasn't enough," I stated, thinking of the other HALOs I'd seen.

The devil waved his hand. "The worshipful donations of her people were pitiful compared to what I could achieve with more HALOs. And so I bound the strongest with adjusted versions that allowed shields and communication, nothing more. Then they made me even stronger by finding sources of suul. Sweet suul, the essence of life and creation."

Rattle. A glance showed the angel gripping the bars, her HALO too bright for me to look long. She must be exerting herself, only to make things worse because all her effort went to the devil. She collapsed to her knees, suddenly weak.

The devil laughed. "Despite starving her of suul, she finds ways to pull it. And then gives it back to me. Her despair is delicious."

"You're nothing but a thief!" I accused.

"She lacked the vision to do great things. I didn't. Her biggest mistake was trusting me."

"I'm surprised you kept her alive."

"Call it nostalgia."

It was Tron who asked, "Why are you afraid of her?"

"I don't fear her," the devil retorted.

"Then why keep her in a cage?" Tron insisted. "If she's so weak and pathetic, why not let her roam free. Wouldn't that be crueler?"

The devil's gaze slewed to the cage then away.

Sensing a sore point, I pressed next, "Afraid of a woman. Kind of ironic. It's probably why he only lets guys be in charge of stuff. He's a coward."

"She can't harm me," the devil boasted and then grimaced as he saw the hole he'd dug. "She won't even try. She knows what will happen if she does." The cage suddenly lowered, hitting the floor with a loud clang that had me bite my cheek. Ouch.

The cage didn't bend at all, but the momentum had tossed the angel to the floor of it.

"You haven't let her out." Tron held him accountable to his boast.

"Those bars aren't meant to be opened."

"Because he's scared of her," I confided in an aside to Tron. Then I clucked.

A universal sound that had the devil suddenly holding a glowing sword of power. It crackled as he approached the cage and then sliced through the bars.

He then never fully turned as he retreated, huffing, "Happy? I told you, nothing to fear."

Yet I would have sworn the devil finally appeared nervous. It made no sense. She remained crumpled in the bottom of the cage, unmoving. Her

HALO a weak flicker that rendered her powerless. But still, the devil appeared wary.

On an impulse, I ran to her side. "Are you okay?"

"She's fine. Move away!" barked Satan.

Instead, I reached out to touch the angel, my hands on her splayed arm, causing me to suck in a breath, as I was given a message. In that second of communication, I saw what I needed to do. And it would hurt. At the same time, pain seemed preferable to death.

Before I could act, a fist of force grabbed me and pulled, dragging me from the open cage and the angel, then lifting me into the air to dangle. I grabbed the fist I couldn't see, my mouth working desperately to suck in a breath.

"Put her down," Tron yelled.

"If you insist," Satan stated, his hand flicking, which, in turn, tossed me. I slid across stone, coughing as I could suddenly breathe. While I pushed to my feet, Tron charged Satan, once more glowing. He slammed into the devil, and they grappled, Tron holding his own, but the sneer on the devil's lips had me wondering if he toyed with my lover.

I had to help, but how? I lacked a decent weapon, and I didn't see my hands doing much damage to a guy with god powers.

A rattling of the bars had me looking at the angel who stood in the door of her cage, eyeing me, reminding me what she'd tried to convey when we briefly touched.

"Give me the token." She wanted the piece of Zilla buried inside me, a last-minute protection given to me by the cantorii. Getting it out would require some digging into flesh.

Big ouch, but the angel in the cage had been insistent, pushing her message to me so hard I couldn't ignore it. I scrambled back to the cage, and as I neared, she extended her hands. I clasped them and stared her in the eye as I said, "Take the token. But be quick. I don't know how long Tron can hold him off."

Rather than reply, she lifted my arm to her lips, as if she would kiss the flesh.

Instead, her teeth sank in.

CHAPTER 17

Slam. He bounced the devil's head off the hard stone floor, to no avail. It did no damage, no surprise since the deity he fought turned out to be both God and the devil, a devasting truth. How could they be one and the same? How had he never suspected? Yes, he'd seen something rotten inside Elyon, but he'd assumed it an illness of the mind. He'd never expected Elyon would turn out to be the personification of evil himself.

Then again, who better than the king of lies to perpetrate the biggest betrayal of all?

They rolled on the floor, and the devil, with his lips tilted in a smirk, gave him a turn smacking his head off the ground. Not that he felt it given he'd conjured a sturdy shield. Back and forth they traded useless blows—for now. He could tell the betrayer held back. Once he tapped into his power, Metatron would be finished. He probably deserved it, given it turned out he'd never been doing good, simply feeding a power-hungry demon.

His sudden dejection led to annoyance from the demon he fought. "I expected more from you. What a waste of potential."

"It would have helped if we had a strong leader." Metatron insulted him right back.

It hit home. The devil's nose huffed smoke, and his eyes burned with baleful malice, but a being of pure evil knew how to strike. "Says the archangel who is responsible for handing over how many flocks to Hell? You abandoned five planets? Ten? More?"

Shame burned inside. How had he not questioned his orders? Why did he blindly obey? At the same time, what else could he have done? God spoke; they answered. They had no way of knowing they worshipped a lie.

It led to him being enraged, which, in turn, filled him with strength as he threw himself at the devil. His hands wrapped around a throat that wouldn't squeeze. Their dueling shields prevented harm, but that didn't stop him from trying.

Metatron punched and wrestled and grunted. To no avail. He couldn't harm the demon, and he felt his strength ebbing as he burned through the suul in his system. His magic... A magic he'd have to replenish on Earth, while the devil simply pulled it from his unknowing HALO slaves.

A hint of blood in the air had them both stilling in their scuffle.

Francesca!

Metatron shoved away from the devil but didn't move fast enough to avoid the kick that sent him stumbling and sliding on his knees toward a bubbling lava pit. Digging in, he slowed his momentum and regained his feet. He turned to see what transpired.

Francesca slumped by the angel's cage, seemingly injured. While he couldn't tell the extent from here, he could smell blood. The angel stood outside her prison, her mouth smeared in a bright wet red that chilled him right through. What had she done to Francesca?

The angel held out a clenched fist and stared at the devil who advanced on her, no longer looking so cocky. He tried cajoling. "Get back in the cage, Gaaya."

Gaaya's HALO flared bright, as did the fist she held out.

"Don't you dare. It will go badly if you do," the demon threatened as he sprinted the last few steps, squinting as the ring on her head got brighter and brighter.

Gaaya lost her blank expression to a wide smile, which grew as the light from her HALO and fist bathed her in radiance. A burning of his retinas forced Metatron to look away.

A soundless concussion went through the room, sending a shiver through him and the floor underfoot. In the distance, a siren went off, and the pools of lava in the room suddenly stilled.

Not a good sign.

On a more positive note, the devil suddenly ceased his advance and even backpedaled from a stretching Gaaya. She rolled her shoulders and dangled her arms. Tilted her head side to side before fixing Lucifer with a grin. She glowed, all over, but as for her HALO? Gone. And that scared the devil.

"Stay away," Satan threatened as she began to advance on him.

"Lucifer, you deceitful demon. There's no point in running. I told you what would happen. Do you remember?"

"Enjoy this minor bout of freedom. It won't last long." A boast that Metatron wasn't sure Lucifer could follow through on. Not with the way he kept retreating.

She spoke as if he hadn't replied. "I promised that when I removed your curse, you'd die. And I always keep my promises." Said matter-of-factly in a dulcet tone that belied the glee in her eyes and steps. The rags she'd worn shimmered into something new, opaque swatches of fabric that shimmered as if reflecting the stars.

"You might be free, but you're weak. I'm the one with the power still from all the other HALOS." Lucifer ceased moving backwards to stand tall.

"Is it more than what I can take from this monstrosity you call home?" Gaaya spread her arms and tilted her head back. "So much potential here that you've left untapped."

"You can't access their energy. They don't worship you." Lucifer sounded more desperate than convinced.

"They don't have to offer it willingly. I can just take. After all, I am the goddess of origin." She took a step, and it shook the very floor. "The mother, the original harbinger of life." Another step and a crack zigzagged from the impact. "If I demand tribute, they will give."

As she stated that, guards finally spilled into the room, six cyclops, brandishing weapons as they charged. She turned to face them, unafraid, the loose fabric of her dress undulating, her hair lifting as well. Her wings flared wide, and what he'd taken for white feathers turned out to be pearlescent scales that reflected and refracted.

Metatron could have stood by her side to help fight, but instead, he ran for the cage and Francesca. His knees hit hard as he knelt beside her slumped body. The blood appeared to be coming from the arm she held tight. Good, she'd applied pressure. He put a hand over hers and dropped his shield to push some of the holy spirit inside into healing her, at least enough that she wouldn't bleed out.

"What happened?" he murmured as he sought to stop the flow, and quickly. The trembling underfoot didn't bode well. Time to leave Hell.

"Gaaya needed the token from Zilla to remove the HALO."

"And so she bit you to get at it." It made sense, even if he didn't care for the bloody outcome. But Francesca would survive. Would Gaaya, though?

She stood in the path of the charging cyclops, a hint of a smile on her lips. Her wings flared out. As she held out her hand, silver limned her shape and beauty danced in her words as she sang, "I am the mother, the hag you call the one-breasted whore. From me came all cyclops. For your betrayal and aiding my captor, your punishment is life." The singsong statement ended, and the creatures collapsed, one by one, clouds of silver rising from their bodies and spiraling for Gaaya. She held her head back, mouth open, arms wide, basking in the silver cloud before absorbing it. By the time she opened her eyes, they'd achieved a slight glow.

Gaaya turned a sweet smile on Lucifer. "I'll be but a moment. Just getting charged up. *Lover.*" The purred statement had Lucifer retreating, one step only before his brash bully side emerged.

"I think it's time for you to go back in your cage." He charged, his hands glowing in a way Metatron had seen during the HALO ceremony. He was planning to collar Gaaya again.

And Gaaya didn't appear to do anything to stop it. She stood, barely braced, half his size. Lucifer slammed into Gaaya, only to grunt when she didn't move. His hands went to slap her flesh, but she grabbed him by the wrists.

She clucked her tongue before saying loud enough for all to hear. "I hear the humans have an expression. Fool me once, shame on me. And now that I'm free, you're dead." She then lifted Lucifer and threw, effortlessly it seemed, but Metatron noted the slight slump in her shoulders. Those cyclops wouldn't have had much suul, and she'd been starving a long time.

It probably explained why she licked her lips when more of the devil's minions poured into his throne room.

She held out her arms and sang, "My children. Give unto me." One dropped then another, but the minions had sheer numbers on their side. At Lucifer's yelled, "Kill her," they went stampeding, which didn't help the floor-cracking situation.

A chunk of it sheared off into a lava pit, taking a soldier with it, the magma burping as he got sucked out of sight. It didn't stop the others from coming. Gaaya remained as calm as before, and with her arms outstretched and a smile on her lips, she welcomed them. A few almost managing to touch before they fell, their silver dust of life feeding her and without her ever laying a hand on their flesh.

By his side, Francesca murmured, "The mother of life is also the devourer of it."

As if she'd heard, the devourer suddenly turned her gaze on them. Metatron tried to not cower before it. Would they now die too? After all, he'd been aiding the devil this entire time. Meanwhile, the true queen, the one real goddess, had been a prisoner.

Her lips never moved, but he heard her voice. *"Leave. Now. This place will soon cease to exist."*

What of you? A thought more than a reply.

"I am going to make things right again." With that, she turned from him and kept turning in search, seeking the devil who had fled.

The angel of death, one more powerful than Metatron could have imagined, stalked after him, going right through solid rock.

Let her exact her revenge. He would do as she suggested. Leave this Hell.

"You feel well enough to walk?" he asked, preferring to keep his hands free to fight if possible.

"Yes. It hurts a lot less. Thanks." She rose and stuck close as they strode for the exit, the ground underfoot rumbling and pitching dangerously. More than a few sirens sounded now, and while more guards peeked inside the room, none entered at the sight of the magma creeping and slopping from its pits. The treacherous path led to him snaring Francesca around the waist and taking to the air, just in time, as the floor suddenly sank into the lava.

They made it across the room to the other door without being accosted. However, they had a long way to go before they reached safety. In good news, the chaos and panic meant no one paid them much mind. The few that did try to step in their path did not survive. Metatron confiscated the sword from one and used it to menace any that thought to get in their path. Francesca kept pace with him despite her injury. Her pallor and stumbling let him know that, while he'd stemmed the flow, she'd lost much blood. He had to tend to her, but he didn't dare stop, not with the way things cracked around them. Gaaya's release had caused a concussion that appeared to be having a dire effect on Hell's shoddy construction.

The tunnel held many demons fleeing the lower areas to the outer. Some carried belongings; others shoved and pushed in panic. It led to some falling into the chasm that suddenly opened in their path, the edges of it jagged, the hot air puffing from it promising the magma to come. Some hesitated at the rift too wide to leap. A few wingless beings tried to jump and failed. The smarter ones waited their turn to cross a makeshift bridge. Those with wings flew across. There were fewer of those than expected, and in their selfishness didn't pause to help those caught on the other side.

Metatron fluttered over, only to be confronted by a demon in guard's livery. The fool dared to bluster, "You're not supposed to be roaming around, angel."

Metatron grabbed the demon and toss him into the rift rather than waste time arguing.

It led to those who noticed giving him a wide berth as they fled. He held Francesca's hand as they rushed past the marketplace with its screams and desperation as vendors shoved their wares into sacks and crates. The forge loomed quiet and empty when they ran through, unlike the bay with its clamoring people, lining the stairs to the gangplanks that gave entrance to the vessels. Everyone wanted to board, but those that could take passengers appeared full. It led to much anger—and desperation.

He totally understood. He didn't know how he and Francesca would escape, especially since the vessel Metatron sought didn't appear to be where he'd left it, the empty spot indicating it must have left.

Here.

The single thought hit him, and he eyed the empty docking clamps still in their locked position.

"This way," he murmured to Francesca. As they made their way, him shoving to create a path, a few turned desperate faces. Alien but not demonic.

Beings he and the other angels had failed. They'd all been duped.

As they climbed the steps to the gangplank, ships began to leave, lifting off with shapes clinging to their sides. Not for long. The force of departure sent them tumbling to die below, even killing some they landed on.

"Where are we going?" Francesca asked as he coaxed her onto the gangway extending into nothing.

"Can't mount a rescue without an escape," he murmured. The camouflage of the scout ship shivered as the door to the vessel suddenly appeared in front of them. It didn't go unnoticed.

Someone yelled, "There's another ship."

A desperate mob would ignore the fact it wasn't a big one. Metatron could take a handful, no more. He prodded Francesca for the door. "Get inside."

"What about you?"

"I need to do something first."

He stood on the gangplank as a male stepped foot on it, brandishing a bundle.

Metatron opened his mouth to tell him to stay back, only the male thrust forth the fabric in his hands to show a tiny purple face. A babe.

"Please. Take my child. Don't let her die."

The selflessness of the request hit him hard.

"Let me have her." To his surprise, Francesca had

emerged from the safety of the ship and stepped forward to reach for the baby. "What's her name?"

"Shira."

More children were passed up, the youngest being offered with thankful tears that wrenched his heart. These parents made the ultimate sacrifice as Hell crumbled around them. Seeing the good that could exist even in this dark place hurt. That they would try to save their young spoke to him. And he wished he could save them all.

But they had room for only a few. He closed his ears to the wails as they had to close the door to the ship. He tried to not feel the guilt that he couldn't do more.

Francesca stood by his shoulder, a babe in the crook of each arm, as the living scout lifted, the many-armed pilot Keeko still at its console, offering him a simple, "Where to?"

When he floundered, Francesca murmured, "Take us home, to Earth."

CHAPTER 18

As the scout lifted from Hell, it offered us a close-up view of the chaos we left behind. The milling and screaming of those who didn't make it aboard a ship. The smoke that began to spiral as equipment caught fire, either from strain or sabotage. More chilling, the chunks of the—what could I call it? Hell didn't fit in the box of planet, meteor, or spaceship, although the latter might be closest. Whatever the definition, pieces of it broke away, spinning off to become space debris. I had to wonder how many contained people remained trapped inside. It chilled to realize it could have been me.

In more positive news, more than a few vessels were speeding away from the wreckage that used to be Hell, some headed for Earth, others to who knew where. Maybe back to the homes they'd been stolen from.

"Sit down," our pilot advised. "It's going to get rough."

"What of the children?" We'd herded them into a small cabin to get them out from underfoot. I held the two babies since the others were barely old enough to mind themselves.

"Dosed into slumber and secured," said Keeko, his hands moving on his console. "Core temperature of Hell rising. Explosion imminent."

Ominous announcement. I did my best to not squeeze the babies I held. As if sensing my trepidation, Metatron snared one from me and cradled it. Damn him for making my dusty ovaries ache.

The final explosion that splintered Hell spewed magma but not fast enough to minimize the building pressure. The shockwave of the blast hit us. The impact propelled us, flotsam tossed in a wild wave, the force of it pressed against me. I closed my eyes, knowing we spun out of control and not needing to see it. The baby I held whimpered, but I could do little to comfort. It was all I could do to hold myself together.

By the time the rolling sensation stopped, I was ready to barf. I held it in. The baby in my arms didn't.

And in the end, I joined little Shira. Luckily, this wasn't the first time Tron dealt with my puke. He led me to the very small cleansing area, where the squirming bundle and I had the sickness removed, along with a foul-smelling bottom—the baby's not mine. I then handed my cleaned baby off to the many-armed pilot, who already held the other, before throwing myself in Tron's arms for a much-needed hug.

A hug that I never wanted to end. Only he set me aside to say, "Let's tend that injury."

I grimaced as he cleaned the bite mark, which, while painful, wasn't life-threatening. I considered it a badge of honor. After all, I'd confronted the devil and lived to tell the tale by setting loose his mortal enemy.

Of more concern at the moment than the devil? Dealing with the eleven children we'd saved and crammed into this small ship. According to Tron, the voyage back to Earth would be several days. I wasn't sure I could play nanny for a few hours, let alone days.

It turned out to not be as bad as expected. Tron helped, as did our pilot, the pair of them more adept than expected with small people who eyed you with giant turquoise or purple eyes. Had to admit, by the time we met up with Zilla, I was kind of attached to a couple of them. But I also gladly handed over their care to the cantorii, who wanted to know every detail.

By the time we'd briefed her, the choir, the US government, the Templars, and every other bloody agency wanting to know what the fuck happened in space, I was ready to collapse.

A gentle Tron tucked me into bed, and I slept long and deep, waking refreshed. I stretched and eyed the sexy angel doing his version of yoga, shirtless and in only a pair of snug briefs.

Talk about yummy. It roused my desire. After all, it had been a while since we'd been intimate, the tiny spaceship not offering the time or privacy for us to be close.

He caught me watching him, and his body stilled. "Good morning." He'd adopted my very Earth expression.

"It will be." I lay back on the bed and crooked a finger.

A corner of his mouth lifted. "Don't you want to eat first?"

"I want you." I wanted to feel that closeness when we had sex. That connection that went beyond the flesh and wrapped around my soul.

He needed no further urging, joining me on the bed, kneeling between my legs and dipping his head for a kiss. His wings extended to give him balance. I dragged him down to me, my mouth mashed against his, my hips grinding. Screw being slow and sensual.

I needed. He divested me of the sleep shorts and shirt I wore. My hands tore his briefs, and I grabbed him tightly and stroked.

He sucked in a breath and growled. "Stop or I won't last long."

Apparently, I wasn't the only one feeling the urgency. I guided him to my pussy, already slick with desire. The head of him parted my nether lips, and I sighed into his mouth as he penetrated, pushing into me and stretching my channel. My hands grabbed his shoulders, and my fingers dug in as he thrust into me, strong and virile. Not just an angel but a man who loved me enough that he entered the bowels of literal Hell to save me.

And now, not only had we saved the world from being ravaged, we'd both survived and could have our happily ever after.

The orgasm hit, and I cried out as I arched, my body rigid as pleasure took me. His own body went still as his cock spilled, pulsing hotly. We collapsed together with racing hearts and happy souls.

And then we got to work because, apparently, everyone wanted to be debriefed again. We finished early enough for a few hours of relaxation, AKA sex and food. Had an awesome night's sleep, followed by morning nookie. My new life. It was fucking awesome.

I should have known our reprieve would be short-lived.

CHAPTER 19

Zilla made the announcement as they ate breakfast. *"Heaven is on a collision course with Earth."*

Metatron wasn't the only one to choke on his coffee.

The dire news could mean only one thing. "Satan escaped." And now plotted revenge.

"Tricky bastard. He must have been on one of those ships we saw fleeing," Francesca grumbled.

Metatron wasn't as sure. Given the ease Lucifer/Elyon moved between the two kingdoms unknown and unseen, he could easily imagine some kind of long-range beaming system. "He must have killed Gaaya before his departure." Because he had not heard of her being aboard any of the refuge ships they'd managed to contact. It could be she'd found a way to blend in. Or more likely she never made it off Hell.

"Poor thing." Francesca's lips turned down.

"The mother isn't dead," Zilla announced.

Metatron frowned. "How can you know?"

"Because the mother cannot die, for, if she does, all life dies with her."

Then where was she? And did it matter? Heaven was on a collision course with Earth. What Metatron didn't expect? How split the world would be on blowing up Heaven, even though its path would slam it into Earth.

Metatron tried to get people to listen, to no avail.

"Not sure why you're worried. You said Heaven isn't armed," President Jane's remark.

"But the devil is dangerous!" he'd insisted.

"You got away," she'd pointed out.

His own choir also had their own ideas on the matter.

"We just need to convince the angels to remove their HALOS and we will render him impotent," Aziel's suggestion.

If they would listen. He had his doubts seeing as how even the pope refused to endorse any action other than a peaceful meeting, and when Metatron tried to explain Heaven wasn't the oasis he expected, the pope called him Judas.

Metatron grew tired of fighting. He'd tried to warn, and when no one would listen, he chose to spend his days loving Francesca and planning for the worst. He'd already spoken with Zilla about evacuating as many as possible if they couldn't stop Heaven from slamming into Earth. He left it up to the cantorii to choose her own passengers, so long as it included Francesca. He, though, wouldn't be part of the group.

The choir that remained had chosen to embark on one last mission. One of atonement and hopefully a chance for survival for everyone else.

Given their objective—stop Heaven even if it had to be destroyed—they brought as many explosives as they could aboard Shard, the scout ship that had begun looking more gray than black since it left Hell. It had also chosen himself a name. Shard, because he claimed to be a piece of something bigger.

When it came to their desperate mission, Shard had volunteered to help so that Zilla could remain behind as the last line of defense.

None of the angels told anyone of their plan. They simply left and turned off all comms. It killed Metatron to not say goodbye to Francesca. But he knew if he told her, she'd try and stop him or, worse, insist on coming. Aziel had done the same with Lilith, just like Elija left behind Cindy-lu. Even Munna and Eoch had found special partners since their arrival on Earth, but they also departed without a word. This was their last chance. They all stood to lose if this failed.

And it would. A handful of angels against

Elyon's remaining army and citizens? In the best-case scenario, Metatron would manage to convince those on Heaven that God and the Devil were one and the same and have them cast off their HALOs. In the worse? They died and Heaven destroyed Earth.

Shard took them there swiftly, Heaven so close even the people on Earth could see it with their telescopes. But there wasn't any panic this time. Apparently, knowing Heaven neared filled them with hope.

"The redemption is nigh."

"Pray for God's forgiveness that you might enter his kingdom."

The humans were convinced of many things, their mortality not being one of them. They thought God had come to save them.

Shard didn't encounter any kind of warning or resistance as it neared Heaven. The impeccable kingdom with its perfect lines and patterned surface lacked any kind of chaos—or signs of life.

During their approach, Metatron scanned as much as he could, even called out on a few communication channels. No one replied. Ruse or something more sinister? He feared the latter.

The oasis where they docked arks, cantoriis, and skiffs was the emptiest he'd ever seen. Not a single vessel remained, and Shard could not detect any signals of them anywhere in the vicinity.

"There is something severely wrong here." Aziel stated the obvious.

"Stick close," Metatron warned.

They kept their steps stealthy, and still their arrival echoed too loud. Heaven had never been so quiet. No singing on high. No cherubs flitting through clouds. The streets of white marble empty of citizens.

They entered homes and businesses at random, finding nothing, no bodies, no signs of violence. It was as if everyone had just up and left.

"Where is everyone?" Eoch whispered, his divinii blade held out in front of him as if expecting an attack.

"It's like they just vanished," an equally haunted-looking Munna replied.

"Let's get to the palace." Metatron led the way to a place as equally bereft, the soldiers by the pearly gates missing, the portals themselves ajar. Their boots echoed loudly, a warning to all they approached. No one challenged their right to enter, and having been called before Elyon many times, his feet knew the path.

They found Lucifer/Elyon in his throne room, splayed on his throne, arms spread wide, his wings torn from him and thrown at random. They didn't need to see the empty eye sockets, gouged clean, the guts ripped from his body, or the blood that soaked the formerly fluffy throne to know he was dead.

"Do you think the angels revolted?" Elija asked, circling the body.

"Seems awfully violent," Aziel noted.

"Does it matter who did it?" Metatron didn't state his theory, that Gaaya got her revenge, but at what cost? He couldn't help but think of all the angels now missing. Had they fed the abused goddess?

"The more important thing is, how do we steer?" Munna, ever practical, asked.

It turned out they couldn't. According to Shard, *"Heaven is no longer alive."* It made sense, though. After all, Heaven had always provided, and in its death, it would now take, since its body, set in motion, couldn't be diverted from its crash course with Earth.

"Guess we have no choice." It was with heavy hearts they set the explosives. This had been their home, and while they'd come prepared to do what it took to stop Heaven's final voyage, a part of them had hoped to avert tragedy and disaster.

At least no one remained aboard. Gathering some mementos of the once wondrous place, they left, triggering the blasts once they'd gone a safe distance. Alas, they'd gravely miscalculated. While a few pieces did separate—the creche where they'd been raised being one building that spun off—the bulk of Heaven remained.

They'd failed, and Earth had less than three days

before impact. Three days of governments vainly firing off missiles as they suddenly realized their folly. Missiles that failed. Despite being dead, some protections lingered. The explosions caused sparkling fireworks in the sky, as the shield around Heaven held.

By the time the choir made it back to Earth, there was only a day left before impact. Not much time to evacuate.

The moment he beamed aboard Zilla, Francesca threw herself into his arms, kissing him then haranguing. "Don't you ever run off to be a hero again."

"Hardly a hero. We failed." His lips turned down.

"Don't be so sure. You weren't the only one working to stop the apocalypse." She appeared smug.

"What did you do?" he asked.

"Used my brain. Ready, Zilla?"

"Ready."

Zilla put herself in Heaven's path and shot a beam of holy light. Stronger than anything he'd ever seen. Potent enough they couldn't watch for more than a few seconds. It took longer than that before the intense laser bored a hole deep enough into Heaven to destabilize its structure. Unlike Hell, it didn't explode but turned to dust. A dust that drifted on galactic winds. Motes that might even make it to some of the flocks on the colony planets, only they wouldn't realize what it meant. They'd have to convey a message that Heaven and Hell had been destroyed, especially to the choirs stationed off Heaven when everything happened.

But that could wait a moment while he hugged the woman he loved. He buried his face in her hair. Breathed in. Breathed out.

They were alive, together, and had a bright future, and a universe to enjoy.

With all kinds of possibilities now spread before him, Metatron started his new life making love to his mate.

EPILOGUE

It had been several years since the destruction of Heaven and Hell. Years during which I'd chosen to travel with Metatron to nearby galaxies, sending out beacons to let others know what happened in our far-away, tucked pocket of space. We didn't say anything about Gaaya in those open messages, but we did keep a lookout for her. Metatron had told me what happened on Heaven, and a part of me worried that she might turn her sights on Earth next. How did you stop an angry goddess?

Years of nothing happening led to that fear lessening, mostly because we had other problems to occupy us. It would seem Earth had drawn attention, first with Lilith's space-faring drones and then the whole Heaven/Hell fiasco. With other cultures—and some alien pirates—showing some interest in our no-longer-hidden galaxy, humanity had to quickly mount a space defense system, to ensure those thinking we'd be easy marks knew to take Earth's Republic seriously.

But having a standing galactic defense force didn't stop a set of really nasty pirates from being very public with their raping and pillaging of a small town in Newfoundland. It backfired on them because it turned out Canadians weren't always very nice. They hunted those pirates down and hung them. It didn't end there. Humanity decided the movies had it mostly right and aliens were bad. As such, an alien ban came into effect that forbade them from setting foot—or tentacle or claw—on Earth. That prohibition included not only all refugees from Hell but the babies we'd rescued and the angels, too. After all that had happened, people were determined to expunge everything they considered alien from the planet.

A good thing we had a friend named Zilla, who, along with her mentee, Shard, took the choir along with as many as could be fit on board—only if they wanted to go, of course. There was a large number, as it turned out, who wanted to take a chance on aliens and a life post-Earth. Aboard Zilla, we travelled not only in safety, but in comfort too as we explored strange new worlds. We saw so many wonders. Planets of water with actual merpeople. Worlds of sand and lizards. Others of bugs. But also places with folks that looked just like me.

Elyon's seeds. Or were they Gaaya's? Didn't matter in the end because we were all free.

Free to live. Free to laugh. Free to love.

When one day a tiny little squirt appeared to join our caravan, I wasn't surprised when Zilla announced, *"Shard and I conjoined our essence to create an offspring."* And thus did Sharla join our group.

She wasn't the only new baby. More than a few bellies rounded on board, including mine, meaning Metatron started treating me like a fragile feather made of glass. I didn't mind. Mostly. I only chafed when we visited the planet of winds, a place of towering aeries and no roads, not meant for those with legs. He left me aboard because of my fragile state.

Imagine Tron's surprise when Zilla beamed me to join him with my splendid set of wings. Great big fluffy ones. A good thing I'd been practicing in secret on board to surprise him. When I arrived in front of him, I didn't immediately plummet, and once he got over his shock, we flew.

Me and my angel, forever on wings of love.

MEANWHILE, *several galaxies and a blackhole away...*

Tamara stood in the crook of Zakai's arm as they stared out through the screen Atlantis provided. A planet loomed, getting larger as they neared.

Despite it not being necessary, Noah pointed. "Behold, Terranovum." A Latin-based name that basically stood for new Earth, a second chance for humanity to start over without the politics and ugliness of the past. To that end, everyone aboard, with the exception of Tamara, Zakai, and Noah, had their memories washed clean of Earth.

They would begin as equals on Terranovum, with none of the prejudice or hate, watched over by their guardian angel, theologian, and the symbiotic ark.

"Are you sure you don't want us to go back to find your brothers?" she asked. "Find out what happened?" They'd gone dark the moment they left, not wanting to leave a trail Heaven or Hell could follow.

Zakai's free hand crossed his body to cup the head of the child sleeping against her shoulder. "I have everything I need right here."

And it turned out to be enough. Humanity flourished on Terranovum, as did the angel who decided to settle among them with his wife and child.

The ark remained in space, orbiting the planet, a moon in the sky as far as the citizens on the surface were concerned. A guardian who wouldn't fail to protect, not with Noah and Atlantis keeping watch. They had a most important task when it came to tending the flock. After all, the goddess had finally returned, and she would need a source of power. To her, they prayed,

Our mother, who freed us from Heaven, hallowed be thy name.

To our kingdom, please come,

Your will has been done,

And the souls we tend are yours for the taking.

AND SO ENDS *this very strange and complex alien angel series that started because of a beautiful cover and then turned into something much more epic than I ever expected.*

Looking for more stories? Check out EveLanglais.com

www.ingramcontent.com/pod-product-compliance
Lightning Source LLC
LaVergne TN
LVHW031538060526
838200LV00056B/4560